Lily took a shaky breath as she walked into the *Latte Mornings* studio. She still wasn't sure why she was there.

When she'd got home the previous night she'd convinced herself that she would forget all about Jacques. Especially since she still felt raw because his interest in her—his kindness to her—had all been a ploy to get her to help him.

She'd told herself she should have known. Her ex, Kyle, had been nice to her once upon a time. It was how she'd fallen for him—and how she'd learned that niceness was never simple.

But still, it stung.

Jacques's dismissal had felt like confirmation that she wasn't likeable. And even though he'd claimed otherwise his actions had shown her the truth. They had amplified all her insecurities and she'd been determined to escape. She'd been determined to show Jacques she was as right for his plan as anyone else was. So she'd kissed him.

It had been impulsive. It had been hot. It had been everything she'd expected from a man with Jacques's undeniable sexiness and charm. But there had been something more too. She remembered the scar above his mouth again, the fight he'd said he'd had with Kyle, and realised it had been *dangerous* too.

It both thrilled and terrified her that she seemed to be attracted to the danger she sensed in Jacques. And, though she wanted to, she couldn't deny that it was part of the reason she was walking into a television studio at six in the morning to pretend to be his girlfriend. She knew this plan was a form of redemption for him.

Dear Reader,

I can happily admit that creating Jacques, the hero of this book, was a bit of a guilty pleasure for me. He's done things he isn't proud of, earned his bad-boy reputation, and is now looking for a way to redeem himself. While bad boys have never been my cup of tea, I can definitely see the appeal of a bad-boy-gone-good—hence Jacques. In fact I'm fairly sure that's the reason I'm a little in love with him myself...

It's also the reason why Lily, my heroine, falls for him. Lily has struggled all her life with insecurities and bullies, and pairing her with a charming and slightly arrogant hero was a pleasure—and probably a tribute to my younger self, who had a lot in common with Lily! It was wonderful to witness these characters grow and defy their pasts. And making sure Lily didn't give in to Jacques as easily as he would have liked was pretty great too!

Jacques and Lily's story is fun and sassy, filled with all the satisfying emotions of falling in love. I hope you love it as much as I do! If you want to get in touch you can find me on Twitter @ThereseBeharrie or Facebook at Therese Beharrie, Author. You can also contact me through my website: theresebeharrie.com.

Here's to happily-ever-afters that sparkle!

Love,

Therese

THE MILLIONAIRE'S REDEMPTION

BY
THERESE BEHARRIE

First Published in Great Britain 2017
By Mills & Boon, an imprint of HarperCollins*Publishers*
1 London Bridge Street, London, SE1 9GF

ISBN: 978-0-263-06953-2

Our policy is to use papers that are natural, renewable and recyclable
products and made from wood grown in sustainable forests. The logging
and manufacturing processes conform to the legal environmental
regulations of the country of origin.

Printed and bound in Great Britain
by CPI Antony Rowe, Chippenham, Wiltshire

Therese Beharrie has always been thrilled by romance. Her love of reading established this, and now she gets to write happy-ever-afters for a living and about all things romance in her blog at theresebeharrie.com. She married a man who constantly exceeds her romantic expectations and is an infinite source of inspiration for her romantic heroes. She lives in Cape Town, South Africa, and is still amazed that her dream of being a romance author is a reality.

Books by Therese Beharrie

Mills & Boon Romance

The Tycoon's Reluctant Cinderella
A Marriage Worth Saving

Visit the Author Profile page at millsandboon.co.uk.

For my husband,
who was the official consultant for this book (and the unofficial consultant for every other). Thank you for making me see that I am more than enough.

For my mother, who taught me that the best way to deal with bullies is to believe in myself and work even harder. Thank you for helping me through it.

And Lunelle, who's always willing to defend me (even when it isn't necessary).
Thank you for your love and support.

I love you all.

CHAPTER ONE

'AND THE SOLUTION you've come up with is *marriage*?'

Lily Newman's steps faltered at the words. Not because she was at an engagement party—her best friend Caitlyn's—where marriage was supposed to be celebrated, but because of the anger that stiffened every word she'd overheard.

There was something familiar about the voice, though not because she knew the person speaking. It was just something in the tone… But that was ridiculous, so she focused on the fact that since she didn't recognise the voice entirely she couldn't be overhearing either of the individuals she was celebrating that evening.

She looked around to check whether she might be caught eavesdropping. Not that she *wanted* to be doing that. She had come upstairs to have some time alone. Yes, maybe it *did* have something to do with seeing her ex-fiancé Kyle arrive with the woman he'd cheated on Lily with. Okay, maybe it had *everything* to do with that.

Because she hadn't wanted to face it, she'd escaped the lavish party Caitlyn's wealthy fiancé Nathan was hosting at his newly purchased home, thinking she might as well explore considering the time she would spend there once her friend was married. But her exploration had ended fairly quickly when she'd heard those angry words from the room she was now standing outside.

'Mr Brookes, we think—'

Brookes was Nathan's surname, she thought, and realised why the man's voice had sounded so familiar. He was one of Nathan's family. Perhaps the brother Caitlyn had told her Nathan had a tenuous relationship with. The one she'd never met and knew not to bring up in front of Nathan after Caitlyn had told her not to. She knew she should give him his privacy, and was about to leave when the man spoke again.

'It doesn't really sound like you were thinking at all, Jade.'

The voice hadn't risen in volume, but Lily felt a chill go through her.

Poor Jade.

'We…we actually *did* put a lot of thought into this, Mr Brookes.' A male voice took over from Jade, though his words were no more confident.

'Then take me through your thought process.'

Careful, Lily thought.

She looked around again, saw that she was still alone, and leaned against the wall.

'We did the research.' Jade was speaking again. 'The file we mailed you has all the results from various avenues—test groups, opinion polls, social media. Yes, you're a successful businessman *now*, but you've done that largely outside of the public eye. People still remember you as the man who lost the Shadows Rugby Club their chance to compete internationally. They remember you as the man who would do anything to win a game, but took it too far in the end.'

There was a pause, and then Jade continued hesitantly. 'And then all the attention was on your suspension, and the partying you did during the year after your last game for the Shadows…'

'You're not telling me anything new.' The words were flat. 'I hired you because I knew that it would be difficult to…restore my image. But I'm doubting my decision now, since you're telling me marriage is the only way I can do that.'

'It's not the *only* way,' the other man Lily had yet to identify said quickly. 'But it's the fastest way. And considering that the buy-out is time-sensitive…' He trailed off.

There was silence for a while, and Lily pushed away from the wall. Guilt spread through her when she realised she shouldn't be listening to a private conversation. Sure, she wanted to know more about Nathan's mysterious brother—if that was who he was—but it was purely out of curiosity. There really wasn't a *reason* for her to listen to Nathan's family's business.

She turned away, forcing herself to act like the confident woman she was trying to be and face Kyle, but she paused when she heard the voices in the room again.

'I shouldn't have asked you to come to my brother's engagement party.'

So he *was* Nathan's brother.

'We can discuss this tomorrow, after the TV interview.'

Her thoughts froze when she realised the man was now walking towards the door, and her legs moved just in time to avoid being caught. She hurried down the passage and turned the corner that led to the stairs…

And then stilled when she saw the man she was trying to avoid walking *up* them.

Kyle.

His date—the other descriptions in her mind weren't

quite as polite—was giggling as he whispered something into her ear. Lily had never bothered to learn the woman's name—why would she need to know the name of the woman she'd caught naked in her fiancé's arms?—but she *did* remember the red hair and petite frame.

It made her pull at the dress Caitlyn had begged her to wear a few days ago. It was too tight, Lily thought desperately. She wished with all her might that it wasn't in a shocking red colour that did nothing to hide the curves Lily had plenty of—too many, in fact.

Her pretend confidence was already dwindling, she realised. And although there was a part of her that told her it was to be expected when she was about to face the man who had broken her down throughout their relationship—who had cheated on her—she had expected more of herself.

It also did her no good to notice how much *smaller* than Lily Kyle's date was. She watched the man she had once thought she loved slide a hand around the woman's tiny waist, pulling her close enough that there was no space between them. They were sneaking away to fool around, she realised, nausea fierce in her belly. How many times had she thwarted Kyle's attempts to do just that with *her* when they were at parties? He hadn't only found a woman smaller than her, Lily thought. She was also the risk-taker Kyle had always wanted and Lily would never be.

In the split second before Kyle saw her Lily decided to take a risk. She wanted Kyle to think that she had been making out with someone upstairs. That the thing she had refused to do with him—the thing he had found someone else for—she was now doing with someone *other* than him.

She would probably think that it was a terrible decision later, but as she fluffed her coiled curls and rubbed her lips together to smudge her lipstick she only hoped one thing—that Nathan's brother had a sense of humour.

'Lily?'

Kyle's voice immediately sent her skin crawling and her heart galloping. She couldn't believe that she'd once found that voice attractive. Now she heard the slime curl around every word.

She lifted her eyebrows. 'Kyle? I didn't see you there. How are you?'

The *of-course-you-saw-me* glint in Kyle's eyes set her teeth on edge and had a small part of herself recoiling.

'I'm well. How are you? I heard you managed to get that bookstore up and running eventually.'

'It's doing really well, actually. My initial investment was quite substantial, as you know.'

Kyle's eyes hardened, and satisfaction pumped through her. But then it gave way to the usual feelings of disgust at the thought of how their relationship had ended. At how she'd compromised her integrity, her dignity.

She ignored the fact that her self-confidence was deteriorating with every moment she spent in his presence.

'You've never met Michelle before, have you? At least not officially.' Kyle pushed the woman forward. 'We're getting married in a few months.'

'Congratulations,' she answered, and though ice stiffened her spine at the woman's cold look she felt nothing else at the news that Kyle was getting married.

That didn't mean relief didn't wash over her when she heard steps behind her.

Not even considering that it might be someone else, she spoke again. 'I didn't think you needed that much time to recover, honey...'

She turned around, and the words tailed off when she

saw her supposed 'boyfriend' for the first time. His skin was the colour of coffee with cream, complemented by dark hair tousled in a style that made her fingers wish they'd been the ones to style it. His dark eyes were stormy, and she realised she had taken a massive gamble with the man—he was clearly still upset about the conversation he had just had.

But the storm cleared immediately after that thought, and was replaced by a look of calm that made her feel even more uneasy. His eyes flickered over her, and then looked at Kyle before resting on her again. The calm then transformed into interest—amusement, too, she thought—with the faintest hint of some secret knowledge that made her skin heat.

He looked nothing like his traditionally handsome brother. His face was made of rugged planes that suggested he had a thousand stories to tell, and just above his mouth was a scar that she could imagine feeling during a kiss.

When the sides of the lips she was admiring curved upwards, she flushed. He might not be traditionally handsome, but he sure as hell was sexy.

'"Honey"? You and Jacques…you're dating?'

Kyle interrupted her perusal, and Lily felt her tongue stick in her mouth when she realised that Kyle *knew* Nathan's brother—Jacques.

You should have thought of that, Lily admonished herself.

She knew that Kyle was here because Nathan worked in Kyle's family's law firm. Nathan loved his job, and hadn't wanted to upset the prestigious Van der Rosses by not inviting the man who would one day become his boss. Caitlyn had assured her it was the *only* reason Lily's ex-fiancé had been invited.

'Yes, we're dating.'

The smooth baritone of Jacques's voice sent shivers down Lily's spine, and she struggled to shake the feeling.

'For how long?' Kyle said, and she turned back to see the smugness disappear.

It bothered him, she thought, her heart accelerating in an instinctual response to Kyle's anger. But then she paused, and told herself she didn't have to be worried about him lashing out.

She didn't have to worry about him at all any more.

'Almost six months now,' she said as Jacques moved down a step to stand beside her. He was a full head taller than she was, and she tried to ignore the awareness that realisation brought.

'Six months?' Kyle repeated, and she saw his eyes flash.

They'd broken up a year ago, and clearly he thought six months was too short a time for her to mourn for him.

'It doesn't feel like six months, though,' Jacques said, and she shifted her gaze to him. 'I barely feel like I've scratched the surface with you.'

So he *did* have a sense of humour, she thought, and smiled. When he responded with a smile of his own her breath caught and she thought something crackled between them. Her heart thudded when Jacques wrapped an arm around her waist, and for a moment she forgot that it was all a game and lifted her hand to brush at a piece of his hair.

'How did you two meet?'

Kyle's voice punctured the tension in the air and she looked at him with a foggy mind. It took her a minute, but when she came out of her Jacques-induced haze she noted the grim set of Kyle's lips. He *really* didn't like this, she thought, and waited for the panic. For that quick rush of trepidation that anticipated that she was about to be put in her place.

But nothing came. And somehow she knew it was because of the easy strength exuded by the man at her side.

'I'd love to tell you all about it, Kyle, but we were up there for far too long.'

Lily shot a flirtatious glance at Jacques, and briefly wondered how deep a hole she was digging when she saw a flash of heat in Jacques's eyes.

'We should probably spend some time with the happy couple. Enjoy the rest of your evening.'

Taking Jacques's hand, she hurried down the stairs, weaving her way through the guests. She only stopped once they were outside on the balcony, and then she immediately let go.

'I'm so sorry about that,' she said hurriedly, her chest suddenly tight.

Just breathe, Lily, it's over now.

'Care to explain?'

There was a slight breeze in the air and Lily walked to the edge of the balcony, turning her face towards the wind. It helped steady her, and when she opened her eyes—when she saw the view in front of her—that did, too.

Nathan's new house stood at the top of the Tygerberg hills in Cape Town, and she could see Table Mountain and most of the city from where she was. It reminded her of how small her problems were.

Even the after-effects of a bad relationship.

'How about we start with an introduction?'

Her words were said a little breathlessly, and she cleared her throat. Nerves had replaced panic, and she glanced around. No one was paying attention to them. That helped.

'Lily Newman—best friend to the bride-to-be.' She offered a hand.

'Jacques Brookes—brother of the groom-to-be.'

He took her hand and it was like touching the coals of a fire. It made her want to break the contact immediately, but he held on, shaking her hand slowly. The heat went up her arm, through her chest...

Before it could move any further she pulled her hand away. 'Nice to meet you,' she said, and folded her arms, constraining the hands that suddenly wanted more of the fire. 'It probably would have been better if that had happened before the whole debacle inside.'

'I don't know,' he answered with a sly smile. 'It was much more interesting than the way I usually meet girls.'

'I'm sure you must mean *women*, because clearly...' She gestured to herself, and then flushed when she saw appreciation in his eyes.

But he only said, 'Touché,' and made her wonder why she'd said those words.

They'd made her sound sassier than she was. As if she was in his league. As if she was used to playing the cat-and-mouse game of flirtation. She almost laughed aloud at the prospect of being in *any* league.

No, she thought as she took in how effortlessly Jacques's muscular body wore his suit. He was *way* too attractive to be interested in her. Someone who looked like him spent time with models and actresses—definitely not with women who had more than twenty-five per cent body fat.

She distracted herself by offering the explanation he'd asked for earlier. 'Kyle's my ex-fiancé—'

She broke off when he lifted a hand, and she saw that his ring finger was a little crooked.

'The one who dumped him a month before the wedding?'

'Yes.'

'I always thought the woman who did that had some balls.'

She smiled. 'Thanks.'

'It doesn't explain why you dated him in the first place.'

It was the same thing she'd asked herself when she'd realised how poorly he'd treated her. But that realisation had only come at the end—when she'd been *forced* to see the truth. She'd been blinded by how charming, how handsome he was at first. And at all the times when he'd switched it on again sporadically throughout their relationship.

But the simple truth was that the blinkers had been kept in place because he'd been *interested* in her. It had been intoxicating—until it hadn't been. And then she'd found him with a naked woman and regained the gift of sight. It had grown clearer with each hour that had passed after she'd ended it. With each phone call Kyle had made. With each threat...

She was ashamed that she'd dated a bully—that she would have *married* him—just because she didn't think enough of herself. She'd dealt with bullies her entire life—she should have known better. And then there was the guilt, the *indignity* of her actions after the break-up...

'Some things you only realise with time,' she finally answered Jacques.

'Touché,' he said again.

She watched him shift his weight from one leg to the other and frowned. The movement was so out of place for a man who clearly had an abundance of confidence. She thought of the conversation she'd overheard, wondered if what she saw was vulnerability, and felt it hit straight at her heart.

No! she commanded herself. She had her hands full with her own problems. Like the store she'd wanted all her life—had sold a piece of herself to start—which was failing. She needed to focus on fixing *that*—on fixing *herself*—before she could even *think* of getting involved with someone else's problems.

And yet when she looked at the sexy man in front of her the resolutions that she'd thought were firmly in place seemed hazy.

'Kyle didn't seem to like you,' Lily said to distract herself. 'Why is that?'

Jacques moved closer, and the breeze brought his fresh-from-the-shower scent to her nose. Her insides wobbled as attraction flowed through her, but she chose to ignore it.

Or tried to.

'We have history.'

Lily waited for him to continue. When he didn't, she said, 'That's all you're going to tell me?'

He chuckled. 'Apparently not.'

He leaned against the balcony's railing.

'Our families run in the same circles, so I'd met him a few times before Nathan started to work for him. Because I knew he was a—' He looked at her, as though checking what her reaction would be, and then continued with a grin. 'Because I knew he wasn't a very nice person, I used to make a game out of stealing his dates.'

Her heart raced. 'But you stopped?'

Something sparked in his eyes. 'A while before you, yes. Unfortunately.'

Her face heated and she leaned against the railing as well, looking away from the view he was facing towards.

She didn't want him to see how uncomfortable he made her. And heaven only knew why she was staying there with him so that he *could* make her uncomfortable.

'Why?'

'Why did I stop?'

She nodded, and he sighed.

'Because Nathan started working for Kyle's firm. Because I stopped going to events he would be at.'

Jacques fell silent, and Lily wondered if he was remembering why he'd stopped going to those events. Had it been because he'd started playing rugby? Because he'd stopped? Had it been during the year *after* he'd stopped?

She folded her arms again when guilt nudged her at the way she'd got the information to wonder those things at all.

'And,' Jacques said after a while, 'because I didn't have time to deal with the punches he tried to throw at me.'

Surprise almost had her gasping. 'Kyle tried to *hit* you?'

His lips curved and her pulse spiked.

'*Tried* being the operative word. It was entertaining for me...painful for him, I imagine.'

'You hit him back?'

'Don't sound so surprised. I was defending myself.'

It took her a moment to process that, and then she laughed. 'I would have *paid* to see that.'

He smiled. 'You could still see it.'

She gave him a look. 'I'm not *actually* going to pay you to hit my ex.'

Jacques laughed. 'It wouldn't cost you much if you wanted me to, but I wasn't talking about that. I saw the way he looked at us when he heard we were together. He *hated* it. So I bet if you and I go into that party right now and pretend to be a couple for a while longer his reaction would pretty much be the same as a punch in the gut.'

She'd barely had enough time to consider his proposal before he'd pushed up from where he was leaning and moved closer to her, sliding an arm around her waist. Her eyes widened and her mouth opened as she drew a quick breath. She watched his eyes lower to it. He only needed to dip his head—it was barely five centimetres away—and she would know if she could *really* feel that scar during a kiss...

He moved his mouth until it was next to her ear and whispered, 'Kyle's watching, so you might want to make that decision quickly.'

CHAPTER TWO

JACQUES COULDN'T DENY enjoying the way the woman he'd only just met shivered in his arms. Or the look her ex—a man he had a *very* low opinion of—was aiming at him. But those things were irrelevant to him at that moment. What *was* relevant was an opportunity to do just as his PR firm had advised. An opportunity that had just fallen into his lap, and would get him exactly what he wanted if he used it properly.

Lily shifted, reminding him that the opportunity wasn't an *it* but a *who*.

'If I say yes, will you let go of me?'

She asked it in a shaky tone, and he looked down into uncertain eyes. They became guarded a moment later, and he frowned, wondering where the spirit he'd admired earlier had gone.

'I'll let go of you regardless, Lily.'

He spoke softly, but forced his heart to harden. He couldn't feel anything for her—including empathy. It would make using her a lot more difficult.

It sounded harsh, even to him, but he knew he would do it if it meant he could redeem himself from the mistakes he'd made in the past. He'd been trying to do that since he'd realised he was only proving people right—

specifically his father—by acting the way he had during the year after his suspension.

The realisation had had him channelling the 'I'll do whatever it takes' motto he'd been known for during his rugby days into building a sporting goods company. Into making it a success.

Now it was. And yet people *still* thought of him as the bad boy who'd beaten up his opponent seven years ago, and it grated him. So when he'd heard that his old rugby club was being sold, he'd known it was an opportunity. He could go back to the root of it all—to where his problems had started.

The irony was that he needed a better reputation to get the club he believed would change his poor reputation. And Lily was the key to that.

'Let's do it.'

The words were said firmly, surprising him after the brief moment of vulnerability he'd just seen, but he simply asked, 'Are you sure?'

'Yes.'

She gave a quick nod, and then moved her mouth so that it was next to his ear, just as he had done to her earlier. It made it seem as if she was responding to his question—something her action made seem suggestive—and he would have appreciated the strategy if a thrill hadn't gone through his body, distracting him.

'We'll have to tell Caitlyn about this. If she sees us and thinks we're together she's going to freak out.'

She pulled back and laid a hand on his chest—an intimate gesture that had his heart beating too hard for his liking.

'That would probably be best,' he answered stiffly.

It took him a moment to figure out whether his tone

came because of the effect she had on him or the prospect of speaking to his brother.

A fist clenched at a piece of his heart as it always did when he thought of Nathan, but he tried to focus on his task. He took Lily's hand and led her through the crowd of people he no longer cared enough about to know to where his brother and Caitlyn were standing.

Holding Lily's hand sent awareness up and down his arm, but he ignored it. Attraction wasn't something new to him. *There's more with her,* a voice taunted, and again he tried to think of something else. But his options seemed limited to things he *didn't* want to think about, and he sighed, realising he would have to face at least one of them.

His brother won, Jacques thought as they reached the circle of people Nathan and Caitlyn were surrounded by. The easy air that Nathan carried around him—the way it translated into ease around people—had always been something Jacques had admired. Sometimes envied. Until he'd realised that people were overrated. One day they saw you as a hero, doing things they admired—the next those very things were criticised and *that* was how they defined you.

But Jacques knew it was also the easy way Nathan approached their less than stellar parents. How he was still in touch with them when Jacques hadn't seen them in years. How he could still want to be a part of their family after all they'd had to deal with growing up…

He stopped that train of thought when he saw they'd attracted Nathan's attention, and with a slight nod of his head Jacques indicated they go to a quieter corner of the room.

'I'm glad you came,' were the first words from his brother's mouth.

'You knew I would.'

Nathan sent Jacques a look that had a lance of guilt piercing his chest. It made him think about how he hadn't seen either of his parents there that evening—*Surprise, surprise,* he thought, despite the relief coursing through him—and he realised it was disappointment, not accusation, that had Nathan doubting Jacques. And that it wasn't exactly *Jacques,* but their whole family.

While Jacques sympathised with his brother, that feeling was capped by the memory of the thousands of times Jacques had warned Nathan to stop *hoping* with their parents. Jacques had learnt a long time ago that it would get him nowhere. His anger about it had ended his career, after all. Had taught him to stop trying. And, since he hadn't seen them in seven years, he figured he'd succeeded in that.

'Congratulations,' Jacques said, remembering that this was the first time he'd seen his brother and his fiancée since they'd got engaged.

He brushed a kiss on Caitlyn's cheek, enjoying the smile that spread over her pretty face, and then went in for the obligatory handshake and pat on the back with his brother.

'While that was both amusing *and* touching,' Lily interrupted with a small smile, 'I know you both have to do the rounds, so we just wanted to tell you we're going to pretend to be dating so that I can make Kyle feel a fraction of what I felt when I walked in on him and her—' she nodded a head in the woman's direction '—naked.'

By the time she was done Jacques could tell that she was out of breath. Which didn't surprise him, since with each word the pace with which she'd spoken had increased. What *did* surprise him was what she had said— that Kyle had cheated on her. While he'd been amused at being roped in to being a pretend boyfriend earlier, he understood why she'd done it now. And he no longer felt amusement over the situation.

There was a stunned silence, and then Caitlyn said, 'Honey, are you okay?'

'I'm fine.' Lily brushed one of her delightful curls from her face. 'We just wanted to warn you in case you wondered. Or got asked about it. And, while we're speaking about that, we've been dating six months. You and Nate introduced us.'

Jacques's lips twitched at the way their story had evolved, but the amusement faded when he wondered how Kyle could have cheated on someone like Lily.

Someone like Lily? a voice questioned, and he realised it sounded crazy. He barely knew her—she might have cheated on Kyle first. But given what he knew about Kyle and the few moments he'd spent with Lily he highly doubted that *she'd* been in the wrong.

His opinion of Kyle dropped another notch, and the temptation to relive the night he had knocked the man out boiled in Jacques's blood. He frowned, wondering where the intensity of his feelings—a mixture of anger and protectiveness—came from. And then he felt his brother's gaze on him, and looked up into a flash of warning.

Since he'd experienced a surge of protection for Lily himself, he understood it. But it singed him to know Nathan was thinking about Jacques's past with women. And it burned to know his brother's warning was on point, considering what he planned to use Lily for.

'You don't have to worry, Cait,' he said, distracting himself.

He knew Caitlyn was the one to win over if he wanted his plan to work. Caitlyn gave him a quick nod, then turned her attention to Lily.

'You know I never liked him—especially after everything...' She trailed off, glancing at Jacques. Then she quickly said, 'I give my blessing for this fake relationship in the name of payback.'

Caitlyn had sparked his curiosity, but it was forgotten when Lily smiled and his chest constricted.

Simple attraction.

He willed himself to believe that when his skin prickled as she took his hand again. And when she looked back with those beautiful eyes of hers to check whether he was okay with it and his heart raced.

He gave her a quick nod, and she started towards the doors that led to the side of the balcony that held the pool. Before he could take more than a few steps with her, someone touched his arm and he looked back.

'Please...be careful with her,' Caitlyn said, looking at him with eyes that reflected her plea.

'I... I will,' he answered, before he could think to say anything else, and the gratitude that shone from her face had his stomach dropping.

He glanced at his brother, saw the frown that suggested Nathan didn't believe him, and his stomach dropped even further. He turned back to Lily, following her until she stopped next to the pool, and tried not to think about the interaction he'd just had. It made him wonder what it was about Lily that inspired the protectiveness he'd seen in the two people he'd just spoken to—the protectiveness that he'd felt himself.

He cleared his throat. 'Are we going for a swim? I didn't bring my swimming trunks...although I have nothing against stripping down to my birthday suit.'

'What?' she gasped, and a smile spread across his face.

'I'm kidding, Lily. Unless...?' he teased, and enjoyed the way red tinted her olive skin.

The colour made him think of the other women he'd dated—he used that term loosely—who spent hours in the sun trying to get that tone. Something told him that Lily would never spend so much time on such a vain endeavour. Not when he was sure the messy auburn curls surrounding her face hadn't been tampered with. When he was sure her beautiful face bore almost no make-up. Her hazel eyes weren't highlighted by mascara or liner. The blush on her high cheekbones wasn't artificial, nor was the pomegranate hue of her full lips.

As attracted as he was to the outside—he took a moment to enjoy the way her body filled out the dress she wore, just as he had when he'd been coming down the stairs—he found himself more intrigued by what the outside *told* him. How many women did he know who would come to an upper-class party *without* plastering their faces with make-up? How many would leave their hair in its natural state when every other woman had hers sleeked up in some complicated style?

Certainly none of the women *he* knew, he thought.

And her reactions to his teasing were so refreshing. Endearing. It made her feel more authentic. And it made her perfect for his plan.

It also made him realise how little innocence the women he'd spent his time with in the past had had. But then innocence wasn't exactly something he'd been looking for in the past. No, he'd been looking to forget the way he'd screwed up his life. And then the public had turned on him—had destroyed him in the media—and he'd begun to wonder what the point of trying was. If they wanted a bad boy, that was what they would get. And they had—for an entire year. The worst time of his life…

'I don't know why I let you fluster me.' Lily's words tore him from his thoughts. 'I know you're teasing.'

'And if I wasn't?'

She sent a look at him that had him smiling.

'Nice try, but it isn't going to work again.'

'It was worth a shot. How else would I be able to see the wonderful colour your cheeks turn when you're flustered?'

She shook her head, and with her bottom lip between her teeth looked away.

Because he saw the very colour he'd been talking about again, he grinned. 'This is fun.'

'For you, maybe,' Lily answered, but she didn't seem upset. 'What did Caitlyn say to you when she called you back?'

'You saw that?'

She nodded, and it took him a few seconds to decide what to say to her.

'She told me to be careful with you.'

Lily nodded again, her face pensive, and then her eyes shifted to something behind him. She moved closer and gave him a whiff of citrus and summer. It was a heady combination, he thought as his body tightened, and he assured himself that that was the only reason for his reaction.

'Our plan seems to be working.' Her curls shook as she lifted her head to look at him. 'Kyle barely seems to be paying attention to his—'

Her eyes widened and she bit her lip again. The prickle in his body became an ache.

'Date?' he offered, to distract himself, but couldn't help the hand that lifted to tuck a curl around her ear.

'Sure—let's go with that,' she murmured, and fluttered those dark lashes up at him.

The ache was replaced by a punch to the gut.

'Why do I need to be careful with you?'

It suddenly seemed imperative for him to know.

'You don't…' she breathed, and electricity snapped between them.

'Are you sure?'

'No.' She shook her head. 'I'm tired of being treated like I'm going to break. My fiancé cheated on me. I was—' She stopped, and there was a flash of vulnerability on her face before it was replaced with a fierce expression. 'You don't have to be careful with me. Treat me as you would any other woman.'

CHAPTER THREE

JACQUES'S EYES FLICKERED down to her lips, and Lily realised how her request sounded. Under any other circumstance she would have been mortified at the implication of her words. Now, though, she *wanted* Jacques to take advantage of the ambiguity. She wanted to be taken advantage of...

'I wouldn't be pretending to be your boyfriend if you were any other woman.'

His voice broke into her thoughts and she blushed at the direction of them, wondering where they'd come from.

'Why are you doing this for *me*, then?'

The heat she'd thought she'd seen earlier in his eyes cooled into an enigmatic expression.

'Besides the fact that you basically forced me to on the stairs?'

She nodded, feeling her blush deepen.

'At first because I couldn't imagine anything better than making Kyle Van der Ross uncomfortable. Now it's because I want to make him jealous.'

He looked at her, and she realised they were having this conversation in an awfully intimate position. She took a slight step back, to give herself some air—and to prevent herself from being distracted by his scent—

but stopped when he placed a hand gently on the small of her back.

It sent her next question stammering from her mouth. 'Wh…wh…why?'

He smiled at her—a soft smile that was in stark contrast to his intimidating masculine presence—and she wondered what she was missing. A man like Jacques wouldn't be interested in *her*. And even if he was the last thing *she* wanted was to get involved with someone who could shatter the self-esteem she had fought so hard for.

The self-esteem she was *still* fighting for.

'He cheated on you, Lily. And only the most despicable of men hurt the women they claim to love in that way.' His face no longer held an easy expression. 'Besides, I *like* helping you. And before you ask me why, it's because I like *you*.'

'You barely know me,' she retorted. It was easier than acknowledging the truth of his words.

'I know that you had the guts to leave someone who cheated on you. I know that you're loyal enough to come to your best friend's engagement party even though you knew your ex would be here. You're innovative—I don't think I know many other people who would come up with the idea of a stranger pretending to be their boyfriend—and you're thoughtful enough to let your friends know about the charade so that they don't get upset. What more is there?'

He grinned, but she couldn't bring herself to respond. Hearing him describe her like that sent a gush of warmth through her body. But it didn't seem right. Not when she was used to harsh words. Not when she was used to people telling her how she should look. How she should be. And from her parents—from Kyle, too, she'd realised too late—how much *better* she could be.

'Fine—you know things about me,' she said, when the silence had extended a tad too long. 'How about you share something about yourself, then?'

'Sure,' he replied easily, and touched her waist to shift her to the left. 'It's easier for Kyle to see you like this.'

Her skin felt seared at his touch, and her thoughts went haywire for a second. And in that second she saw herself pressed against Jacques, kissing him until she no longer knew who she was.

She shook her head, thinking that she didn't know who she was *now*. This woman having inappropriate thoughts about a man she barely knew was definitely not her. She'd never gone that far—even in her most lonesome of days.

When she'd been overweight it had been easier to avoid attention. And even when she'd lost some of her weight she had still been too afraid to put herself in a situation where men might hit on her.

It had been on the one night Caitlyn had convinced her to go out—in their final year at university—that she'd met Kyle. He'd been the first person to treat her like a woman, and not like 'the girl who lost weight'. His attention had been flattering, overwhelming. She'd fallen hard, and had been swept into his world like a commoner into a castle.

His offhand comments about her looks—he hadn't seemed to have a problem with her weight, but her hair, her face, her clothing were still fair game—hadn't mattered when he could make her feel like the most beautiful woman on the planet with one look. His suggestions as to how she should act, what she should say, how she might do better had been irrelevant when he was treating her to fancy dinners, to expensive gifts.

'What do you want to know?'

Jacques was watching her, and her face heated even at the thought of him knowing what she was thinking.

'How'd you get the scar?'

He frowned, as though he wasn't sure what she was talking about. And then his hand lifted and he rubbed his thumb over the scar. Lily was hit with the desire to do the same, and she clenched her hand, determined not to be caught in this attraction between them.

'I was in a fight.'

'Kyle?'

He smiled, though his eyes were hooded.

'He didn't land a punch that night. No, there have been other fights.'

His eyes glinted dangerously, and her knees nearly went weak.

What is wrong with you, Lily?

'Next question. What do you do?'

'I own a sporting goods company.'

'What does that entail?'

'Well, there's a shop where the public can buy sporting equipment, but mostly we do bulk and international orders.' He slanted a look at her. 'You've never heard of Brookes Sporting?'

'Hard to believe, isn't it?'

He smirked. 'Just a little.'

'And that's what you chose to do after your rugby career ended?'

There was a beat of silence before Jacques asked, 'How did you know I played rugby?'

She only then realised she wasn't supposed to know that.

'You expected me to know your company, but not that you played a popular South African sport? Besides, I'm sure Nathan mentioned it a while ago...' She trailed off when she saw he wasn't buying it.

'Really? The brother who didn't think I was going to come to his engagement party told you I used to play rugby?'

'Would you believe me if I told you I used to watch you play?'

'No.'

She sighed. She was going to have to tell him the truth.

'I overheard your conversation earlier, Jacques. I'm really sorry.'

That explained how she'd known he would follow her lead when they'd spoken to Kyle, Jacques thought. It also meant she had heard Jade and Riley's suggestion, which put his plan to convince her to be involved at risk.

'Is eavesdropping a hobby of yours?' he asked slowly.

'I didn't mean to,' Lily replied primly. 'I was upstairs because I saw—'

'Kyle and the cheater?'

She nodded. 'And when I walked past the room you were in I heard the whole marriage thing...'

So she *had* heard it, he thought, but soothed the faint trickle of panic by telling himself that she didn't suspect he wanted *her* involved. She wouldn't have agreed to his suggestion to continue the charade of their pretend relationship at the party if she did. And then Jacques would have lost the opportunity to ensure that all the wealthy people who formed part of his brother's social circle— including Lily's ex-fiancé—saw him and his 'new girlfriend'.

The rest of his plan had originally involved them leaving together at the end of the night. It would have just been for coffee—though the party attendees wouldn't have known that—and he would have suggested their pretend relationship continue for just a while longer. But this new information meant he needed to speed up that plan...

'Why don't we get out of here?'

Her eyebrows rose and her cheeks took on that shade of red he liked so much.

'Together?'

'Yeah. We can grab a cup of coffee.'

'Why?'

'I like you, Lily.' Though he'd meant the words to convince her to have coffee with him, he found that he genuinely meant them. Something tightened in his stomach at the knowledge. 'I also think there's nothing more you'd like to do than to get out of here.'

Her face had changed when he'd said he liked her, and though he couldn't quite read it he thought there was a trace of uncertainty there. As if she didn't believe what he said. The tightening in his stomach pulsed, and for the first time he considered how manipulative his plan was. Sure, it wouldn't hurt Lily—but it wouldn't benefit her either. It was entirely for *his* benefit.

But you helped her, too, a voice in his head reminded him. That made him feel better, and because he couldn't afford to dwell on why he should reconsider he chose to focus on that.

'You're right.' Lily's expression was unreadable. 'And buying you a coffee is probably the least I can do to say thank you.'

She was setting boundaries, he realised. Letting him know that she was only accepting his offer because she wanted to say thanks. He wasn't sure why that bothered him, but he didn't have time to ponder it.

'Are you sure you want to leave, though?' she asked.

She looked inside to where Nathan and Caitlyn were standing.

'I don't think Nathan expects me to stay longer than I already have,' he said, ignoring the guilt.

'Do you want to say goodbye?' she asked softly, and he looked down to see a compassion he didn't under-stand—and didn't want—in her eyes.

'I don't want to interrupt them.'

She watched him for a moment longer, and then nod-ded.

He reached for her hand, thinking about how easily he could feign affection with Lily and yet struggle with women he was much more familiar with. His skin heated when her fingers closed around his, warning him that his plan might have complications he hadn't considered.

But as he made his way through the crowd of people with Lily he knew that those complications would be worth it when the Shadows Rugby Club was his and he could help place them in the international league. If he could do that it would make up for the fact that he'd *cost* them their place in that league seven years ago.

When he felt like being kind to himself he told him-self his actions that night of the championship game that should have determined that place had come from anger. From pain. That night had been the last time he'd seen either of his parents, too. Not a coincidence, consider-ing that *they'd* been the reason he'd got into a fight with a player who hadn't deserved Jacques's attention. Who wouldn't have got it if he hadn't uttered those same words his father had before Jacques had arrived at the game...

'You're such a disappointment.'

The memory of that night still plagued him—still scarred him—but if he could pull off his PR company's ridiculous plan maybe he would finally find some peace.

Maybe he would finally be able to put it all behind him and move on.

'Do you have somewhere specific you'd like to go?' Lily asked once they were outside.

He watched her pull her coat tighter around her, saw her look out around the private estate his brother's house was on, and realised she was nervous.

'I'm not going to kidnap you, Lily.'

She looked at him. 'I know. And I'm going in my own car.'

Smart girl, he thought, even though disappointment lapped at him for reasons he didn't understand.

'My office is pretty private.' He saw something in her eyes, and said, 'You'll be safe, Lily. I promise to be-have myself.'

My future depends on it.

She tilted her head, as though she was considering his words. 'So let's have coffee somewhere more neutral, then. I know a place…'

CHAPTER FOUR

'THIS IS *NEUTRAL* for you?'

Jacques joined Lily in front of her store, and looked pointedly at the sign that said 'Lily's' above the glass entrance.

'Relax,' she replied, though the way her heart was beating told her she was probably saying it to herself.

'We're just stopping here for the coffee—then we can take a walk down the beach. It's not too busy this time of night.'

'I usually let a woman take me out for dinner before I do romantic walks on the beach, Lily.'

Her hand froze on the door at his words, and it took her a moment to hear the store's alarm beeping. She hurriedly entered the code, trying desperately to come up with something to say. But her mind only formulated excuses—not the sassy comeback she'd hoped for.

You should have known it wouldn't last, a voice mocked her.

And though she wanted to deny the words she couldn't. She'd thought it was a *good* idea to bring him back to her store and then to walk on the beach. She'd feel better in a familiar place, she'd told herself.

But being in that familiar place had snatched her from the fantasy world she'd been in for the past few hours.

The world where she'd flirted as though she were in a thinner body. As though she had all the confidence in the world. As though she wasn't trying with all her might to value herself.

'This is nice,' he said, breaking the silence. 'It's a coffee shop and a bookstore?'

'Yeah. I love reading and I love coffee, and a lot of the people I know do, too. So I thought it would be pretty great to have a place where you could relax and do both. And, of course, there's the view.'

She was rambling, she knew. A combination of nerves at Jacques being there and the defensiveness she always felt when she spoke about her store.

Her parents' warnings echoed in her head—as did their urges for her to do something more *respectable* than being a store-owner—and she shook it off. She had more pressing things to worry about at the moment.

'Do you have any preferences for coffee?'

'Black, no sugar.'

She busied herself with the task, and for a few moments there was silence.

'You have good taste.'

The milk she was pouring spilled onto the counter. 'Wh...what?'

'I assume you decorated the store yourself?'

She nodded mutely, refusing to look at him in case he wore that amused expression again.

'It's the perfect décor for a shop like this.'

She'd gone with a blue and white colour scheme, to complement the view of the sea that stretched endlessly through the glass entrance. White bookshelves held as many books as she could fit in them—old and new—and lined the walls on either side of the shop. The wooden tables and blue-cushioned chairs were homely, comfortable—exactly what she'd been going for when she'd decorated, though she knew she'd spent hopelessly too much on them.

But she only worried about that when she did her accounts and saw how many negative numbers they had.

'Thanks,' she said, making quick work of the cleanup before handing him his coffee in a takeaway cup. She cleared her throat. 'We don't have to...to do the walk. I just thought it made sense...'

'I was teasing, Lily.'

The smile on his lips made her stomach flip. And then there were even more gymnastics when he lifted her chin.

'You know—that thing I do so I can see you blush?'

She took a step back. 'You mean the thing I shouldn't let fluster me?'

'Exactly.'

She couldn't help a smile at his quick answer. 'How about we take this to the beach?'

She left her coat and her shoes in the store, and a few moments later they were walking on the sand together.

'It's beautiful, isn't it?' he said, looking out to the water.

Waves crashed against the sand at his words, and the reflection of the full moon on the water shimmered, as though thanking Jacques for the compliment.

'Yeah, it is. I remember going on holiday to Johannesburg when I was younger. I refused to go again when I realised there was no beach.' She shrugged. 'Something about a beach just—'

'Calms you?'

'Yeah.' She glanced over. 'Did the same thing ever happen to you?'

There was a bark of laughter. 'That would have involved my parents actually *taking* us on holiday, so no.'

The words surprised her, and if his silence was any indication they had surprised him, too. She wanted to press him—for reasons she didn't want to think about—but before she could Jacques jogged a few paces ahead of her. Lily watched as he threw his empty coffee cup into a nearby bin, and in a few quick movements climbed onto a large boulder.

He grinned down at her when she reached him. 'Join me.'

'Up there? In this dress?' She shook her head. 'I'll pass.'

'How about that one?' Jacques nodded at the boulder next to the one he was on. It was smaller, but she still didn't see herself up there.

'I don't think you understand, Jacques—'

She broke off when he jumped down next to her, threw her coffee cup into the same bin—despite the fact that hers had only been half-empty—and took her free hand.

'Come on—it'll be a good place to talk.'

Helpless to do otherwise, she let him lead her to the next boulder, but stopped when they reached it.

'I don't see how this is going to work.'

'Like this.'

She felt his hands on her waist, and realised his intentions too late—he was already lifting her.

'Oh, no, Jacques,' she gasped. 'I'm too heavy—'

But she didn't get a chance to finish her sentence since her feet were already on the smooth, cold granite of the boulder.

A few moments later, Jacques joined her. 'Did you just say that you were too heavy?'

He barely sounded winded, and it took Lily a while to find her words. She was too busy wondering whether she'd overestimated her weight or underestimated his strength. Since she didn't live in a world where the former was ever a reality, she settled on the second.

'I guess not,' she finally answered him.

'You think you're heavy?'

'I…well… Kyle wasn't as strong as you are,' she finished lamely.

He gave her a strange look, but didn't say anything. Instead he offered a hand, gesturing that they should sit. She ignored the spark that zipped through her at the contact, and snatched her hand back as soon as she was sitting.

'Thanks for agreeing to have coffee with me,' he said when he settled down beside her.

'It was the least I could do after you helped me with Kyle. Even if you *did* throw most of mine in the bin.'

'Sorry…'

Jacques smiled apologetically, but something on his face told her there was more.

He confirmed it when he said, 'I actually wanted to talk to you in private because…'

He took a breath, and she felt a frisson of nerves deep inside.

'I was hoping you would do a little *more* than just have coffee with me.'

'What do you want?' she asked stiffly, hearing a voice mocking her in her head.

Did you really think he was being nice to you because he liked you?

'Nothing we haven't already managed to pull off.' He paused. 'I'd like you to pretend to be my girlfriend.'

CHAPTER FIVE

IT SOUNDED SILLY even as he said it—more so when he saw the look on her face—but he ignored the feeling. *This* was the point of continuing the charade for so long. This was the point of asking her out for coffee.

It shouldn't matter that the easiness they'd shared this past half an hour—the ease responsible for that slip about his parents—had dissipated.

'Are you sure you just want me to pretend to be a *girl-friend*?' she asked quietly.

'Yes. We've done a pretty good job at convincing Kyle. A few more people wouldn't hurt.'

'"A few more" isn't quite the number, though, is it?'

Wondering how she knew, he answered, 'Fine, it's a lot more than a few. But you won't actually be *on* television. I just need the people at the studio to know you exist, so when I mention you on air it'll be believable.'

'What are you talking about?'

'*Latte Mornings*. I have an interview on the show tomorrow morning.' He frowned, realising now that they weren't on the same page. 'What are *you* talking about?'

'I heard your conversation, remember?'

She looked straight at him, and if her words hadn't surprised him he might have acknowledged the way his stomach tightened in response.

'You need a wife, right? Someone who will make you more...palatable to the public for some business deal you're working on?'

'Hold on.' He took a deep breath. 'You don't get to make assumptions about things you overheard—out of context, I might add—in a private conversation.'

Her cheeks flushed, and the spirit that had had her looking him in the eye earlier faded as she averted her gaze. 'I'm sorry that I eavesdropped, Jacques, but I... I can't be your *wife*.'

'I'm not asking you to *marry* me, Lily.'

'Then what *do* you want from me?'

'I just want you to pretend to be my girlfriend. You may have overheard that I'm not entirely willing to marry someone to get the public to like me.' *Not if I don't have to.* 'But you gave me the idea tonight that I could pretend to have a nice, respectable girlfriend and that might have the same effect.'

'And that's the real reason you wanted coffee?

'Yeah. It isn't that much to ask, considering that I did the same for you tonight.'

He shouldn't feel bad about this. He shouldn't have to defend himself.

So why was he?

'And maybe if you'd asked me straight I would have agreed. But instead you just told me to continue the charade for a bit longer—which *now*, of course, I realise is because you wanted to test whether it would actually have an effect, and not because you wanted to annoy Kyle—and then "coffee".' She lifted her hands in air quotes. 'You manipulated me.'

'And what *you* did wasn't manipulation?' he snapped back at her, guilt spurring his words. The picture she had painted reminded him too much of his father.

'I didn't manipulate you,' she answered primly. 'I told you why I did what I did. I was honest with you as soon as I had the chance to be.'

He shrugged, pretended her words didn't affect him. 'And I'm a businessman. I know how to capitalise on opportunities.'

'This isn't an *opportunity*,' she said coldly. '*I'm* not an opportunity.'

'Of course not.' He said the words before he could think about how they might undermine the cool exterior he was aiming for.

'Then stop treating me like one.'

She was right, he thought, and then remembered that she'd said if he'd been straight with her maybe she would have agreed.

'You're right—and I'm sorry for the way I went about this.'

She gave him a look that told him she didn't entirely trust his words. That look combined with the wounded expression just behind the guard she was trying so desperately to keep up, made him feel a stab of guilt.

He *had* manipulated her. And he should know, since he'd witnessed his father manipulating his mother for his entire childhood. Somehow the man had made his wife believe that telling their children they were disappointments, failures, was normal. That raising them without the love and support parents were supposed to give was acceptable. And his mother, so desperately in love with a man who had only wanted her for her money, hadn't believed she'd deserved more.

That her children had deserved better.

When Jacques had finally managed to convince his mother to kick his father out it had only taken his father a few minutes to change her mind. And now Jacques regretted it. The trying. The hope. The fact that he'd done it on the night of the championship.

It had been the reason he'd been so easily provoked into the fight that had got him suspended for three years. That had lost his team their chance to be a part of the international league they had fought so hard to play for.

It was why buying the Shadows now was so important. And why he needed to make amends with Lily.

'Would you give me another chance to ask you to be my girlfriend? My pretend one, of course.' He wasn't sure why he clarified it, but it made him feel better.

'If you tell me why you need a pretend girlfriend, yes.'

He nodded, and forced himself to say the words.

'Seven years ago I was suspended from playing rugby.' It took more strength than he'd thought it would to say the words. 'I got into a fight that cost my team a championship game and the chance of playing in the highest league they could play in.'

She interlaced her fingers and rested her hands in her lap. 'What was the fight about?'

'It doesn't matter,' he answered, because it was true.

'The scar?' she asked, tapping at her lip.

He wondered what intrigued her so much about it, but only nodded. There was a beat of silence before she spoke again.

'It must have been important if it cost you something that clearly meant so much to you.'

Maybe it had been important to him once—the chance of a family without his father. Now Jacques thought he'd been fighting over something that hadn't been worth nearly as much as it had cost him.

'It doesn't matter," he said again. 'It's only the effect the entire thing had on my reputation that does.' He paused. 'I heard recently from a few business associates that my old rugby club is going to be sold soon, and I want to be the one to buy it. Except I've been told that some of the club's biggest sponsors will pull out if it's sold to me. The only way to prevent that, it seems, is to build a more...*positive* reputation.'

She stared at him. 'You're seriously telling me that people care that much about your reputation?'

'Apparently.'

'And the only thing you did to get this negative reputation was have a fight?'

'One that lost my team the championship *and* an opportunity.'

'Yes, of course—but that's *it*?'

He hesitated. 'Well...'

Jacques really wasn't interested in rehashing the details of the year when he'd spiralled into the depression that had damaged his reputation even more.

'Well...?' Lily repeated, a single brow arching in a way that made him forget the tension of the conversation they were having.

'The year after I was suspended I spent a lot of time... Well, I spent some time on a self-destructive path,' he said once he had steadied himself.

'What does *that* mean?'

'I...' He'd hoped his explanation would be enough. 'I told myself that I didn't care what people thought about me, and I did exactly what I wanted to.'

And yet, ironically, it had been caring about what people thought that had *made* him act that way in the first place.

When she didn't speak after a few moments, he found himself asking, 'Why aren't you saying anything?'

'What did that entail?' she said in lieu of a reply.

He tried to formulate an answer, but nothing he could say would make him look good.

'I can't help you if I don't know the truth, Jacques.'

'Parties. A lot of swearing at journalists. Women.' He ran a hand through his hair, wondering how telling her all this intimidated him more than tackling the largest of men on a rugby field. 'What more do you want me to say?'

'So you were a bad boy?' she asked.

He cringed. The term brought memories he would rather ignore.

'I thought people *loved* bad boys.'

'Maybe,' he conceded, and then considered her comment. 'I think people only love bad boys as an idea. Something or someone far away from them. But they definitely do not when a bad boy, say, wants to date their daughter.'

She tilted her head, and one of her curls sprang over her forehead.

'So you're saying that people don't want you to buy a rugby club because they love the club too much?' She looked at him. 'They don't want you to "hurt their child"?'

He opened his mouth to protest, thinking her oversimplified explanation couldn't possibly be the reason he was in his current dilemma. But after a few moments he realised that that was *exactly* what was going on.

'Pretty much, yeah.'

'And if you have a girlfriend…?'

'If people see that I have a respectable girlfriend—a steady one—maybe they'll like me enough to trust me with the Shadows again.'

She frowned, and he waited as she processed his words.

'You really think that would work?'

No, was his first thought, but he said, 'I trust the people who work for me. If they say having a wife—or a girlfriend—people like will make them see me more favourably, then I believe them.'

There was another pause, and then she asked softly, 'How do you know people will like *me*?'

The hesitancy in her voice scratched at the protective instincts he'd locked away seven years ago.

Look where that had got him with his mother.

'Because you're likeable.'

Her curls bounced as she shook her head. 'No, I'm not.'

'Based on whose evaluation?' When she didn't reply, he said, 'Lily, you asked me to be honest. How about you do me the same courtesy?'

She looked down at her hands and he saw another glimpse of that other side of her. The side he'd seen when she'd claimed to be too heavy for him to lift her onto the boulder. It hit him harder than he might have anticipated, and he clenched his fists to keep himself from comforting her.

He barely knew the woman, and even if he did there was no way he wanted to get involved with her troubles. He'd purposely steered away from relationships to avoid being lured into protecting someone as he'd had to protect his mother. And Lily's insecurities reminded him a little too much of the woman he hadn't seen in seven years.

And yet when Lily answered him he found himself forgetting his own warning.

'I had a…a difficult time growing up. Didn't have that many friends. And then a failed relationship…'

The vulnerable look on her face twisted his heart.

'I mean, *that* must say something about my likeability.'

He watched her face change into an expression that

told him she'd said more than she'd meant to, and then the guard slipped back up again. It took him a moment to figure out how to respond.

'You have Caitlyn. And Nathan. They love you.' He paused. 'And *I* like you, Lily.' He said it again, to make her see that someone who didn't know her as well as Caitlyn and Nathan could like her too. Again, he found that he meant it. 'And you can't blame yourself for what happened with Kyle.'

She tilted her head. Didn't meet his eyes. 'Actually, I can. I didn't see him for what he was. I *let* him treat me poorly. I—'

'Stop!' he said harshly.

Seeing the surprise on her face, he forced himself to calm down. But Lily was doing exactly what his mother had done with his father—blaming herself, making excuses. It had always made his blood heat, just as it did now.

'Don't make excuses for him.'

'I'm... I'm not,' she stammered. 'I just meant that—'

She broke off when she looked at him, and he realised he hadn't schooled his face as well as he should have.

'I'm sorry. I just—'

The tone of her voice sucked all the anger from him. 'You don't have to apologise,' he said softly, unable to help himself as he took her hands into his.

She nodded, and the colour that had seeped out of her face started to return. His stomach turned, and he realised Lily wasn't the right person for his plan. She was too vulnerable...too fragile for him to bring her into the public light.

It had nothing to do with the fact that she awoke feelings in him that he had buried the night he'd written his parents off. Feelings that reminded him of when he'd fought for his mother. Feelings of protectiveness, of tenderness—feelings that had no place in what he wanted to achieve...

'*I'm* the one who should be apologising,' Jacques said, his decision made. 'I shouldn't have asked you to do this.'

'What?'

'You're not the right person for this, Lily.'

He saw her face blanch, was about to comfort her, but then thought better of it. He moved his hands from hers, immediately missing the warmth, and stood.

'I don't think that being in the public eye together is right for either of us,' he finished lamely, but he could tell that under her stony expression she was upset.

'Okay,' she said hoarsely, and then cleared her throat. Her voice was much stronger when she spoke again. 'You're probably right. No one would believe we were together anyway.'

She pulled her legs up and he could see she was contemplating how to stand without his help. He offered it anyway, and she accepted reluctantly—and again, so she could get off the boulder.

With each step back things between them grew more tense. Something inside Jacques grew more unsettled—so much so that he sighed in relief when they reached the pathway leading to her store.

'Thank you for your help with Kyle today,' she said primly, and each stilted word had his chest tightening.

'I was happy to help.'

It sounded strange to him to be so formal after what they'd just spoken about, but he didn't know how else to respond. He didn't even know why her words left him with an ache in his chest.

Silence stretched, making it feel as though there was more distance between them than the few centimetres from where she stood on the pathway and where he stood in the sand. The silence was heavy with disappointment, and it shook him more than he cared to admit. Perhaps because he'd lived with it hanging over his head his entire life. The disappointment that he would never live up to expectations he didn't know.

Like when he'd been hailed as the best player the Shadows had ever had and it hadn't impressed his father.

Heaven only knew what the man wanted from him—or from Nathan, for that matter, since even Nathan's law career had made but a blip on Dale Brookes's radar. But even disappointment implied caring. It implied that his father felt enough for his children to *want* them to achieve certain things. Since Jacques was sure that wasn't the case, maybe it was his own disappointment that his father didn't love them that was bothering him...

He shook his head. *Where had that come from?*

'Jacques?'

'Yeah?'

'I think I'm going to kiss you.'

He barely had time to process her words before her lips were on his.

Heat seared through him and his lungs caught fire.

He heard her intake of breath, realised that she felt the same.

Except that while his reaction had been to deepen the kiss hers was to pull away.

They stood like that for a moment, his hand lightly on her waist, both of hers on his chest. He felt them shaking against him and only then realised that his body was shaking too. Her eyes were wide, and the flush on her cheeks was caused by an entirely different reason than his earlier teasing.

'I'm so sorry,' she breathed, aiming her striking eyes at him.

Stealing his breath. Stoking his desire.

'I didn't mean to—'

This time he interrupted her with another kiss.

His arms went around her waist and he pulled her closer, lifting her from the path until she stood with him on the sand. Somewhere in his mind it registered that the romance of taking a walk on the beach that he'd teased her about earlier shrouded them now—that their first kiss was now on a beach in the moonlight. But then he stopped thinking, consumed by the magic of her mouth.

She tasted like strawberries just ripened. Smelled like a warm day in spring. Something inside him softened at the sensations that came with her kiss. She responded hungrily, deepening it. He heard a groan and realised that it had come from him. Because she was making him forget where they were—who he was and what he had to lose—he fought to slow the kiss. He hoped it would lessen the tension, the urgency, that had built between them.

But his attempt was a vain one, only succeeding in making him want more.

In making him *need* more.

He pulled away from her, his breathing as shaky as hers, and forced himself to take a step back. Forced himself not to be charmed by that just-kissed look on her face. He ignored the fact that her expression was like that because *he* had kissed her—deeply and thoroughly—and reined his emotions in.

'We shouldn't have done that.'

She looked up at him, her hand freezing midway to touching her lips, and he watched her fingers curl into a fist.

He felt as though his heart was right in the palm of that hand.

'No, we shouldn't have.'

She bit her lip, and his body yearned to go back to what they had been doing. It took him a moment to realise that she was doing it to keep herself from saying anything.

'We probably won't see each other after this, so it doesn't matter.' He felt like an absolute jerk saying it— even more so when he saw her flinch. Her words about no one believing that they would be together played in his head again, and he wondered at them. Wondered why he thought his words now had proved the truth of that to her somehow.

'Good luck with the TV show tomorrow. I'm sure everything will work out.'

She turned her back on him and hurried down the path before he could respond. And because he wanted to give her—and himself—some time to process events, he waited before following.

But that time wasn't nearly enough for him to process everything that was going on in his mind. To figure out why his actions that night had shamed him. Especially since they weren't actions he would have been ashamed of at any other time.

Or with any other person.

It was Lily, he realised. Something about her made his actions feel...unethical. *Manipulative*. He hadn't thought he was being manipulative. Or perhaps, more accurately, he hadn't cared. At least not until she'd called him on it. And that kiss had only complicated things between them. He worried that it would affect the self-confidence she had so much trouble with.

Which was why this was for the best. He didn't need to

worry about someone else's self-confidence. He needed to focus. He'd worked too hard to make up for his past to be distracted by a woman. Besides, as much as Lily intrigued him, she needed someone who would take care of her. Someone who would be patient with her insecurities, who would appreciate the spirit that covered them.

Someone who didn't have a million hoops to jump through before people saw him as decent.

And that wasn't Jacques.

It was for the best, he thought again, and didn't examine why it didn't feel like it. Or why realising that he wouldn't see Lily again any time soon made him feel more empty than the task ahead of him.

CHAPTER SIX

LILY TOOK A shaky breath as she walked into the *Latte Mornings* studio. She still wasn't sure why she was there. When she'd got home the previous night she'd convinced herself that she would forget all about Jacques. Especially since she still felt raw because his interest in her—his kindness *to* her—had all been a ploy to get her to help him.

She'd told herself she should have known. *Kyle* had been nice to her once upon a time. It was why she'd fallen for him—and the way she'd learned that niceness was never simple.

But still, it stung.

Jacques's dismissal felt like confirmation that she wasn't likeable. And even though he'd claimed otherwise his actions had shown her the truth. They had amplified all her insecurities and she'd been determined to escape them. She'd been determined to show Jacques she was as right for his plan as anyone else.

So she'd kissed him.

It had been impulsive. It had been hot. It had been everything she'd expected from a man with Jacques's undeniable sexiness and charm. But there had been something more, too. She remembered the scar above his mouth again, the fight he'd said he'd had with Kyle, and realised it had been *dangerous.*

It both thrilled and terrified her that she seemed to be attracted to the danger she sensed in Jacques. And, though she wanted to, she couldn't deny that it was part of the reason she was walking into a television studio at six in the morning to pretend to be his girlfriend.

She knew this plan was a form of redemption for him. She'd read articles about what had happened during his last game. Watched the footage. She'd seen the absolute anger on his face. Felt the danger of it settle in her throat when she hadn't been able to tear her eyes away.

Her instincts told her that that fight *had* mattered, despite Jacques's claims otherwise. And the more digging she had done, the more she'd become convinced of it. The internet was full of what had happened after that fight. His red card…the suspension. The year he'd said he'd been 'self-destructive'. The pictures.

She didn't know Jacques very well, but she knew the man in those pictures wasn't the same person she'd spoken to the night before. The man in those pictures was broken. Completely so. But the man *she'd* met hid that brokenness well…

It had all fuelled her urge to help him. And in an effort to avoid the thought that she wanted to help only because she was attracted to him, she'd realised she could do with *his* help. She *needed* it if she wanted to save the store she'd opened six months ago from going under. And she *had* to save it—or the guilt that anchored her heart to the soles of her feet most days would be for nothing.

Pretending to be Jacques's girlfriend would give her a platform where she could market her store from. To get more customers, to get more income and pay more bills. *That* had been the real reason—at least the biggest one—

she'd got up at four-thirty, got ready and driven almost an hour to the television studio.

Because she couldn't fail with her store. She couldn't fail at her dream. And she sure as hell couldn't prove her parents right and fall even further short of their expectations.

But her steps faltered when she saw the two security guards at the entrance of the studio. How was she going to get past them?

If she tried to talk her way through—told them she was Jacques's girlfriend—she would just seem like some crazed fan. In fact *all* her options would make her seem like that. And even if they did believe her, how would she verify it? She couldn't call Jacques, since she didn't have his number. The only thing she had of him was the memory of the heat their lips had sparked when they kissed. And she highly doubted *that* would get her through...

Her courage failing, she turned to leave.

'Lily?'

She turned back at the sound of her name, her heart beating so fast it might have been sprinting to win a race. Jacques stood just behind the security guards, a cup of coffee from the barista next to him in his hand. Her eyes greedily took him in, which in no way helped to slow down her heart-rate. She'd managed to underplay her attraction to him in her memories, convincing herself that she'd exaggerated his good looks. Even the pictures she'd seen on the internet hadn't swayed that conviction.

Now, though, she was forced to admit that she couldn't have exaggerated Jacques. She had never seen someone look *that* good in jeans and a T-shirt, though the black leather jacket escalated the look. Along with the mussed hair, she saw another reason for his bad-boy nickname...

But the confusion on his face distracted her.

'Hey, babe,' she said, and wondered if the 'babe' was too much. But when she saw the way his eyes widened, she decided to commit.

'I'm *so* sorry I'm late. Can I go in?' she said to the security guards, and after getting a brief nod of confirmation from Jacques they let her through. She walked up to him, steeled herself against the attraction, and gave him a quick kiss.

'I didn't think you were coming,' Jacques said, the slight shock in his eyes at her presence and at the kiss almost immediately cloaked.

'I changed my mind. I didn't want you to go through this alone.' She took the coffee from his hand and sipped. It was strong, without any milk, and she had to force herself not to spit it out. 'Do you think we could get another?'

Amusement crept into his eyes, and he nodded. A few moments later he was back, this time with a coffee that had milk in it—he'd taken note the night before, she thought—and two sachets of sugar.

'Let's swap, *honey.*'

The drawl he used made her lips twitch.

'I know how much you like hot coffee.'

She thanked him as they exchanged their coffees, and then forced herself not to react when he put an arm around her shoulders and the smell of his cologne filled her senses.

'You want to tell me what you're *really* doing here?' he said under his breath as they rounded the corner to where they shot the morning show.

'I'm paying back a debt,' she responded in the same tone.

'You didn't have to.'

They were in the main studio now, and she was briefly

distracted by the busyness of the set. She had never been on one before, and it was a little overwhelming.

She forced her attention back to Jacques, moving in front of him to make it look as if they were talking intimately. In reality, she just wanted to be out of his arms.

'I know, but this is important to you, right?' He gave her a wary nod and she continued, 'So let me do this. It's not like it's real. What's the harm?'

He studied her for a moment, and then he said, 'Thanks.'

'No problem.' When their gazes locked and something sparked she took a step back and looked at her watch. 'What time are you going on?'

'Seven-thirty.'

She nodded, stayed still for a moment. And then, when the silence grew a little awkward, she said, 'It wasn't until I got here that I realised I wouldn't be able to get in. So… thanks for getting yourself some coffee.'

She smiled thinly at him, and turned away before she could become ensnared by his magnetism.

'Mr Brookes? We're ready for you in Hair and Make-up.'

Lily watched as the young woman tucked her hair behind her ears when Jacques directed his attention to her.

'You can follow me,' the girl said quickly, and turned. But then she realised that Jacques wasn't following. 'Is there a problem?'

'No…not unless my girlfriend has to stay out here?'

The girl's eyes widened, and her black hair whipped from side to side as she looked at Lily and then back to Jacques again.

Though it was strange hearing Jacques call her that, something fluttered inside Lily at the thought. Something that was lined with pride, with satisfaction. With a thrill.

She tried to ignore it.

'Um…sure, you can both follow me.'

Decidedly less confident, the girl led them to a room that looked exactly like the rooms Lily had seen in movies. Jacques was settled into the chair in front of one of the mirrors, and she sat herself on the couch opposite the chair. The man who was doing Jacques's make-up was tall and lanky, with bright green spikes all over his head. There was barely an introduction—though she did learn the make-up artist's name was Earl—before he began putting foundation on Jacques's face, and she couldn't hide her smile.

'Something amusing you, Newman?'

She met his eyes in the mirror and found her smile broadening. 'Why would you think that, Jacques?'

'Maybe because of that ridiculous smile on your face?' He closed his eyes as he said it to allow Earl to put foundation around them.

'Fine—you caught me. But I was only thinking how wonderful it is that I don't have to do your make-up for you today. Thanks so much, Earl.'

Earl glanced over at her, his expression amused before he schooled it and got back to work.

'You're ruining my reputation, Lily,' Jacques growled, and Lily felt a thrill go up her spine.

She loved the banter, the easiness of the conversation they were sharing. It seemed that having a conversation with Jacques as his pretend girlfriend was a lot easier than having one as his friend. Although, to be fair, she could hardly call whatever she and Jacques shared a *friendship*. Perhaps 'alliance' was a better word.

'Are you going on with him?' Earl asked as he put some wax on his hand and vigorously rubbed it through Jacques's hair.

'No, no,' she said quickly. 'I'm just here for moral support.'

'And you're doing a great job, babe.'

She shot Jacques a look that she hoped told him he was laying it on a bit too thick, but Earl didn't seem to notice.

'You two are quite sweet. Not who I would have pictured you with, Bad-Boy Brookes, but maybe that's a *good* thing.'

Earl pulled at a few more strands of Jacques's hair, then nodded. 'You're as ready as I can make you. I'll go check how long it'll be before you have to go on. I'll be right back.'

He had barely walked out of the room before Lily spoke.

'That nickname has quite a ring to it.'

Jacques got out of the chair and came to sit next to her. He knew just as well as she did that he was too close, but since he seemed to want it that way Lily refused to indulge him by moving away. She just shifted her weight so that she was leaning to the other side.

'It's not one I'm proud of.'

'Nor should you be, if all the articles I read last night were true. Particularly the one that had the headline: *Bad-Boy Brookes's Year of Debauchery.*'

He turned towards her, the look in his eyes dangerous. 'I'm not sure what's more disturbing. The fact that you looked me up, or that you've mentioned that horrible headline.'

She flushed, but refused to look away.

'I had to know what—or who—I was agreeing to support. And I'm glad I did it. I now understand why you need me.' She paused, sensing the tone of the conversation would change if she continued talking about the things she'd learnt the night before. Unwilling to lose the easiness between them, she said, 'Besides, now I'm prepared if some woman tries to gouge my eyes out.'

'It's not *that* bad,' Jacques said, hoping his blasé attitude would mask his embarrassment.

'Yeah, you're right. I mean, the articles didn't make it sound bad *at all*,' she teased. 'Only about ninety per cent of them used the name "Bad-Boy Brookes" when referring to your personal life—the other times they used it to refer to your willingness to do whatever it took to win a match. And it was also *only* used if you were seen partying with more than one woman over a single weekend. So you're right,' she said again. 'It really wasn't that bad.'

She stood, and Jacques's eyes moved over her. The jeans she wore highlighted the curves of her hips, and he stood quickly so that his eyes wouldn't be drawn to them any more. Not that it made him uncomfortable. He had always been the type of man who appreciated the female body, and he wasn't afraid to show it. Except that Lily… Well, she wasn't the kind of girl who inspired the lust he was used to.

His eyes travelled over her body one more time, and he felt the result of it in his chest, his gut, and then his body. No, he thought again, not the type of lust he was used to at all…

'But then, of course, there was that photo shoot.'

Her eyes widened, her cheeks glowing with that wonderful colour he'd grown to like so much the night before, and he grinned.

'Which one? My agent at the time had me do quite a few.'

'The underwear one,' she said in a high-pitched voice , and avoided his eyes.

His smile grew broader. She hadn't intended telling him she knew about that, he thought. So why had she?

'Yeah, that was at the peak of my career. One of my favourites. Body didn't croak then like it does now.'

'Are you fishing for compliments?'

She still wasn't looking at him, and he took a step closer.

'Only if you have them.'

'Somehow I think your ego can handle it if I don't offer them to you.'

'Maybe my ego, but not my heart. I need to hear my girlfriend compliment me. Just once.'

Her lips twitched, and she brought her eyes back to his. 'You *know* you look just as good now as you did then. Even though I haven't seen you in your underwear recently.'

'We could change that.'

The joking air between them immediately turned into a sizzle. He hadn't intended to say the words, but he hadn't been able to stop them when she'd spoken. And damned if he didn't mean them. He could see it as clearly now as he had during their kiss last night. The chemistry, the attraction... He wanted it more than he could say. It was almost as if he...*needed* it.

The thought jolted him, and he took a step back. Forced himself to take control again.

'Is it going to be a problem for you?' he finally said, to change the subject.

'What?'

Her voice was a little breathy—just as it had been after their kiss—and he had to steel himself against the desire.

'My dating history?'

She shook her head quickly, causing the curls she had tied up at the base of her skull to bounce.

'Of course not. It's not like we're *really* dating. I have no emotional investment in this whatsoever.'

Her face had gone blank with the words, and for the first time since he'd seen her that morning he wondered why she was there. *Was* she paying back a debt?

He searched her face for a clue that there was more, but saw nothing.

And that had his instincts screaming.

There was something else—something more—but he wouldn't know what until he asked her.

Before he could, they were interrupted.

'Mr Brookes, they want to go through your questions one last time.'

Earl had come back, and with one last look in Lily's direction, Jacques walked out through the door.He forced himself to focus on what he was there to do, and went through the questions he'd previously been emailed with the producers one last time.

He knew his PR firm had given the studio those questions, which was why he'd agreed to this appearance in the first place. It was also why neither Jade nor Riley was there yet. He was confident enough about his answers— answers they had coached him through—to have them there only for the interview itself.

He knew the questions off by heart by now: how was his business going? Particularly his international expansion? Did he have any news about his personal life?

He hadn't had much of an answer for that when they'd first spoken about it, but now he would casually mention his relationship with the lovely Lily Newman, and send her a loving look on camera, after which the host would go on to talk about his past rugby career.

Did he miss it? Did he regret the way it had ended?

Since he did, he would say so, and the sincerity of

his words—according to his PR firm—would be a great segue into his plans for buying his old club. Hopefully seeing him in a stable new relationship, doing a popular family show would boost his image enough that the club's sponsors wouldn't pull out if he bought it.

But he didn't want to spend any more time thinking about the hoops he had to jump through to get people's approval. When he was finished with the producers he walked out of the room—and paused when he saw Lily.

Her arms were folded over a loose red top, a patterned white and red scarf perfectly accessorising the effortless look. She looked a little out of place, he thought, and watched her brush one of her tight curls from her face. It didn't seem to matter that the curls were tied at the nape of her neck. They found a way to frame her face regardless.

She turned to him, smiled , and his heart slowed, nearly, *nearly* stopping. His lungs constricted and he felt as if he'd been kicked in the stomach.

It took a moment for him to recover. The smile on her face disappeared and she took a step forward, but he raised a hand and waved her away, not sure he could have spoken to her if she had come to face him.

What just happened? an inner voice asked, but he shook his head, unable—unwilling—to answer that question. He couldn't afford to. Not minutes before his interview.

And yet when he was called on to the set he had to actively *force* himself to focus on what he was about to do.

He dismissed the insecurity that threatened, reminding himself that he was good at playing games. He'd made an entire career of it, hadn't he?

He could pretend to have a girlfriend, and he could pretend to be someone the public wanted him to be. The way he played only mattered if he didn't score the try, he reminded himself, and no matter what happened he *would* be scoring this try. He *would* be the one to buy his club.

It had saved him from the anger he'd felt at home—had given him an outlet for the frustration he'd felt with his family. But when he'd realised his family wasn't worth it he'd let that anger control him. He'd let it ruin the thing that had always given him meaning. Purpose. But he would make up for it—for the mistakes he'd made before he'd known any better.

'Welcome back to *Latte Mornings*!' David, the host of the television show's sports segment, spoke the moment the producer gave the signal. 'Today's guest needs no introduction. He is one of our biggest rugby legends, who earned respect during his rugby career because of his phenomenal talent. Mr Jacques Brookes. Thanks for being here, Jacques.'

Game on.

'Thanks for having me.'

David went through the questions Jacques had prepared for, only going off-script to make a joke or to comment about something Jacques had said. He didn't once mention Jacques's suspension, which was a relief, since Jacques had worried about that before the interview. Now, though, Jacques was more concerned about the questions regarding his personal life. He wasn't sure he wanted to know why that was the case...

'So, Jacques, tell us about what's going on in your personal life? Are you still breaking hearts?'

David laughed, and for a moment Jacques wanted to wipe the smile off David's face. *Why* would the man remind people of one of the things Jacques wanted them to forget?

'Well, actually, I've been dating someone I think may

be the one.' He looked over at Lily, smiled, and watched as a pretty flush covered her cheeks.

He was still astounded at the fact that something that simple—that natural—could wind his insides with attraction.

David raised his eyebrows. 'That wasn't the answer I was expecting, but that's great. How long have you two been together?'

His mind blanked for a moment, and his accelerated heart-rate suddenly had very little to do with his attraction to Lily.

'Er...six months?' He glanced at Lily, and she nodded and smiled.

He felt steadier. He'd remembered that six months was how long she'd told Kyle they had been together, so the timing would be consistent in their world of pretence.

He realised that his answer had sounded unsure, so he laughed and looked back at David. 'I was just making sure I got it right.'

'Of course. We wouldn't want you to get into trouble.'

David smiled at the camera, and Jacques resisted the temptation to roll his eyes. He didn't care much for David's sometimes over-the-top media personality, but he knew it got the ratings, so he ignored it.

'Tell us a little more about your girlfriend...?'

David's eyebrows rose again, and Jacques answered, 'Lily.'

'Lily. What a beautiful name.'

David smiled over at Lily, and when Jacques's eyes followed he saw her return it with a shy smile of her own.

'Tell us more about her. What does she do for a living? How did you two meet?'

Jacques wasn't sure how long he sat there, his brain telling him that he should have anticipated this line of questioning *before* he'd mentioned her. Suddenly he re-alised he knew nothing about her except the little she'd offered—and that wasn't nearly enough to maintain the pretence.

Gears shifted in his head, and he forced steel into his gut as he tried to resist the decision his mind had already made. He *had* to do this, he thought. It was the only way he wouldn't destroy his plan with his faux pas.

'I'd love to tell you more about her, but actually I think this would be a great opportunity to introduce her to the public. Lily, could you come over here, please?'

CHAPTER SEVEN

PLEASE TELL ME I'm dreaming, Lily thought when Jacques called her over. It certainly seemed like one of those horrible dreams—going on a live television show that almost the entire South African population watched, unprepared. Especially with everyone on set looking at her expectantly.

She felt someone touch her back, and then the coat that had been in her hands was replaced with a microphone and her feet were moving, one at a time, until she was under bright lights and next to Jacques.

Up close, she could see something in his eyes that she couldn't place her finger on, but it didn't matter when she was pretty much living her worst nightmare.

'It's *lovely* to have you with us, Lily.'

David broke the silence, and his eyes told her he was as surprised—possibly even as annoyed—as she was at her being on camera.

'Thank you,' she said softly, and it took Jacques moving the hand that held the mike for her to realise she hadn't spoken into it. Feeling the heat in her face, she cleared her throat and repeated the words into the mike.

You have to stay calm, Lily, she told herself. *Be confident. This is your chance to do exactly what you came here for.*

'Am I in trouble?' Jacques asked, breaking the tension her little fumble had caused, and he casually put his arm around her waist, pulling her closer.

She couldn't deny that it calmed her—which she might have appreciated if *he* hadn't been the one to put her in this position in the first place.

'Definitely!' she answered through numb lips, and resisted looking around when she heard a chuckle go through the studio.

'Is this the first time he's done something like this, Lily?' David asked her, and she idly thought that he must have recovered from *his* shock.

'Yes. And the last time, too, if I have anything to say about it.'

Another chuckle went through the studio, and she felt herself relax slightly. She *would* survive this, she thought, and then she would take her time and enjoy killing her pretend boyfriend.

'We've been pretty private for the most part.'

Jacques spoke up, and she looked down at his smiling face. Noted that the smile was more apology than amusement.

'Which is why there hasn't been anything on social media? Or in the gossip columns, for that matter?' David asked, and drew Lily's attention to the fact that in the world that they currently lived in, relationships were all over social media. And, since Jacques was a public figure, there should have been *some* sign of their relationship somewhere.

Jacques's hand around her waist tightened, and she wondered whether he could tell that she was beginning to panic.

'I think when you have something this special you don't really want it to be in the public eye.'

It would have been a sufficient answer, but Lily found herself saying, 'And since I knew that Jacques was a public figure, and I'd heard about his…his past, I wanted to take it slow and keep it between us for as long as possible. I guess that will end after today.'

David smiled at her, and then sobered. 'And his past doesn't bother you?'

'We all have pasts, David. They make you the person you are. But they aren't the entirety of what defines you. Jacques is one of the best people I know. He works harder than anyone. His business ethic is impeccable. He does so much for the people he cares about, and his charity work—' which she'd read about only a few hours ago '—clearly shows that he doesn't need to know those people personally. If I had let whatever had happened in his past affect my answer the day he first asked me out I wouldn't ever have got to know the other sides of him.'

There was a long pause after she spoke, and she looked down at Jacques to see warmth in his eyes. Her cheeks grew hot again.

'Well,' David said eventually, 'it really does seem like you know a different Jacques to the man we're used to. But that might not be a *bad* thing.' David winked, and then continued, 'We have to go to an advertisement break now, but when we come back we'll talk to Jacques a little bit more about that past we've just touched on.'

When they were off the air Lily's legs began to shake. A delayed reaction, she thought, and was incredibly grateful that it hadn't happened while they were still live. Before she knew it Jacques's arms were around her, drawing her into a hug while keeping her steady, and she wondered if he had sensed her instability.

'Thank you,' he said.

His sincerity sent a shiver through her, and she folded

her arms around him so that their display of affection didn't look strange.

But she didn't respond, unsure of whether the mike he still had pinned to his top was on and if anyone would hear her say what she really wanted to. She drew back after a moment, her body prickling with awareness even though she wanted to kill him.

'All this attention has made me a little shaky. I think I'll wait in the make-up room, so you can't call me back on air again.'

Lily made sure that there was a lightness to the tone she used as she spoke, making it sound teasing and not like the warning it really was. But when she looked at Jacques she saw acknowledgement of her real intentions.

She took a deep breath and walked to the make-up room, aware that people were now watching her. She pretended not to notice, and breathed a sigh of relief when she saw that no one was in the room. She closed the door behind her, locked it, and then sank onto the nearest couch.

Her hands were shaking, she realised, and curled her fingers into her palms to stop them from making her seem like she wasn't calm. Even though no one was there, and even though no one would see her panic, she still felt the compulsion to pretend not to be vulnerable.

It was a defence mechanism she had developed to survive the bullying at school. And it was one that had kept her from seeing the person Kyle had really been. From seeing what their *relationship* had really been. Because if she could pretend everything was okay, even to herself, then surely it would be. It *had* to be.

But that had never been the case. For her younger self being overweight had meant bullying from her peers. And being an introvert who didn't know what she wanted for the longest time had meant her parents had never understood her. How could they when they were extroverted, successful professionals who'd always known exactly what *they* wanted?

Her solution had been to pull back, to be someone no one would notice. That was why Kyle's attention had been so flattering. But then he'd tried to make her believe that who she was wasn't enough. And because it had been so easy to believe him, it had taken seeing him with another woman to realise that she *was* enough.

No, she thought, that wasn't true. It had taken seeing him with another woman to make her realise that she *should* be enough, and that *she* needed to believe it.

She'd been doing a pretty good job of it, she thought, until she'd gone on live TV unprepared and all the insecurities had come rushing back. Now everyone would be watching her, judging her. She looked down at the clothes she was wearing and started to shake again. They made her look even frumpier than she usually did, and the confidence she'd had when she'd chosen them washed away.

All the reasons she'd had for pretending to be Jacques's girlfriend didn't seem to matter any more. Especially when she realised she hadn't even had the chance to promote her store when she'd been on air. All she had done was boost Jacques's ego even more.

But wasn't that the reason he'd brought her on the show in the first place?

She took a few more deep breaths to calm the anger pumping through her veins and walked to the door, avoiding the mirrors in the room so that she didn't have to be reminded—*again*—of how terrible she looked. When she opened the door Jacques was standing there, hand in the air, ready to knock. She plastered a smile on her face, not wanting the sacrifices she'd already made to be undone, and brushed a kiss on his cheek.

'How did the rest of the interview go?'

She forced cheer into her voice and slipped her hand into Jacques's, gently pulling him towards the exit. She assumed since he was there that his interview was done, and she didn't want to stay any longer and pretend she loved a man she wasn't even sure she *liked* at that moment.

'Great.'

Jacques walked with her, though she could sense the resistance in him. They didn't speak for the rest of the short walk to the exit, but Jacques stopped before they could walk past security.

'I have to stay and meet with Jade and Riley. The PR firm reps.'

She nodded, remembering their conversation last night—though it seemed a longer time ago—and brushed another kiss on his cheek as goodbye.

Hopefully for ever.

'Will I see you for dinner later?' he asked, threatening her hopes of never seeing him again. But then she realised that she *wasn't* really his girlfriend, and that this was his attempt at seeing the non-girlfriend Lily again.

And *that* she could refuse.

'I'm working late tonight, honey—remember? You can call me later.'

She waved at him and walked out of the studio, knowing full well he didn't have her number.

CHAPTER EIGHT

'YOU ARE SO lucky I had a deadline this afternoon or I would have called earlier.'

Lily briefly closed her eyes at Caitlyn's irate voice on the phone and locked the front door of the store. It was just before seven, and normally Lily would have taken the store's accounts outside and enjoyed the sound of the sea lapping against the pier and the laziness of Friday evening as she worked.

But today she'd exposed enough of herself to the public.

'I'm not sure I would use the word "lucky",' Lily replied, gathering her things. She just wanted to get home, soak in the bath and forget the mistakes she'd made that day.

'Oh, trust me, you're definitely lucky,' Caitlyn disagreed. 'But that luck has run out and now I want to know exactly what's going on with you and my future brother-in-law.'

'There isn't anything going on with me and Jacques.'

'Really?' Caitlyn demanded. 'Because I'm watching a clip of you defending his past right now. It currently has four hundred thousand views.'

'Cait,' she said wearily. 'Please. I can't deal with snippiness today.'

Lily wasn't surprised her friend had called, demanding answers. She'd already had to deal with her mother's hurt because Lily hadn't told her she was dating again. And by 'deal with' Lily meant 'lie to', since she couldn't possibly tell her mother it was all a charade. She'd managed to talk around it, but that conversation alone had taken up a substantial part of her energy.

But then she'd had to conjure up more for her work day. Because as soon as she'd walked in Terri and Cara, her staff, had demanded why *they* hadn't known. And then people had begun to recognise her, and the store had grown busier than it had ever been before.

'I'm sorry, Lil. I'm just worried about you. You barely know Jacques. Hell, *I* barely know him.'

'I know. I *know*,' Lily repeated more definitely. 'I'm sorry for snapping. It's just been a…a long, long day.'

'Don't apologise.'

Lily could almost see the hand her friend was waving her apology away with.

'At least not to me. Besides, I keep telling you that you don't have to say sorry for bringing the fire. I love it when you do.'

She paused, and Lily sensed her hesitation over the phone.

'Will you tell me what's going on now?'

Lily sighed, and quickly explained everything that had happened in the past twenty-four hours. The only thing she left out was the kiss—she didn't need Caitlyn to remind her of how much she had messed up, and that was the part she was most embarrassed by.

Caitlyn didn't say anything when Lily was done, and her heart pulsed. Her silence was out of character, which meant that Caitlyn wanted to say something she knew Lily wasn't going to like.

'Cait, just tell me what you're thinking.'

'I don't want to…' Caitlyn sighed. 'Fine. Look, I just want you to be careful, okay? I don't really know that much about Jacques, and even when I pressed Nathan about him last night he wouldn't tell me any more than he already had. I just… Well, I don't think he's the person you should move on with. Especially not after Kyle.'

Lily felt annoyance, but pushed it aside. She didn't know why she'd felt it in the first place.

'I'm not moving on with Jacques. This…it's pretend.'

'Are you sure?'

She waited a beat, and then answered, 'Yes.'

'And if you go on with this pretence you'll be fine with all the attention?'

Lily knew Caitlyn wouldn't be her best friend if she didn't know everything about her—well, mostly everything, she corrected, thinking how she'd never told Caitlyn about the way things had really ended with Kyle. But it irked her that her friend knew just where to hit.

'Actually, I take that back. You *have* to be fine with all the attention. You're in this now. You have to keep this illusion going until Jacques's deal is signed, and perhaps even after that.'

Though she desperately wished that Caitlyn was wrong, the feeling in the pit of her stomach told her that her friend was right. She'd known it the minute she'd got that call from her mother.

'I'll figure it out,' Lily breathed, and heard Caitlyn sigh again.

'Just be careful.'

'I will be. Thanks.'

There wasn't much to say after that, and when she'd said goodbye Lily locked up and made her way to the parking lot. She kept her jersey tight around her, despite the early summer heat, and kept her head down. She didn't want to be recognised. Not only because she'd had enough of it that day, but because she didn't know what to expect if one of Jacques's more devoted fans found her.

'Lily.'

Her first instinct was to grab for the pepper spray in her handbag. But though it took her a moment, she recognised the voice.

Jacques was leaning against the car that was parked next to hers. He'd changed his T-shirt from white to blue, abandoned the leather jacket. She felt a flash of disappointment, but shook it off.

'Hi...'

His deep voice rumbled, and her train of thought was derailed. And for that reason, she said, 'No.'

'No, what?'

'No, I'm not interested in whatever you're here to say.'

'Give me a chance.'

'No.'

She shook her head and walked past him to the driver's side of her car. A hand closed over her arm.

'Can we go somewhere private to discuss this, before we draw an audience?'

She knew he was right—that people would recognise him and then perhaps her sooner or later—but she couldn't bring herself to agree.

'We don't have anything to discuss. I did what you asked. Debt paid. Now we can move on.'

'Lily, please. I just need a few minutes. *Please.*'

Her heart softened, though her mind urged her to stay strong. For a minute she struggled between the two. But one look at his face had her sighing.

'My flat is twenty minutes away.'

'Mine is ten.'

She frowned. How had he always been that close to her and yet had only now managed to disrupt her life?

'Fine, I'll follow you.'

Lily was grateful for the short drive, since it didn't give her enough time to indulge her feelings about going to Jacques's flat. So she ignored the slight churn of panic in her belly. Ignored the rapid beat of anxiety in her chest. She'd experienced them often enough with Kyle to recognise the signs of anticipating an argument.

Instead she focused on her breathing. And as she parked her car in front of the sophisticated building in Jacques's secure estate she gave herself a pep talk. But she didn't speak in the elevator they took up to his flat. She didn't comment when he let her in and the first thing she saw was Table Mountain. When the first thing she heard was the crashing of waves.

Jacques put on lights, though it was only just beginning to grow dark then, and she got a better view of the glass that made up one side of his flat. Part of it was a sliding door, she realised when he opened it, and took a step closer. It looked out onto the beach, and the steps leading down from the balcony of the flat went directly to the sand. Having specifically rented her shop at the beachfront for its calmness, she appreciated Jacques's choice. Even though he probably didn't really live there, she thought, looking at the inside.

Grey laminate floors stretched across the open-plan room. Soft white furniture was arranged in the living room to face the spectacular view, with a light brown carpet and white dining room set just behind it. The kitchen was next to that, designed in white and grey to match the colour scheme of the entire flat. Lights beamed softly in the roof above the living room and kitchen, and an intricate fixture hung over the dining room table, illuminating it intimately.

It looked like the homes she'd seen in magazines—visually beautiful, glossy, and so very perfect. Except it didn't *feel* like a home. It didn't have the cosiness a home with a view like his should have.

'You're upset because of the interview today.'

It wasn't a question, and she braced herself for the inevitable.

'You already seem to know the answer to that.' She saw the confirmation on his face. 'Why am I here, Jacques? For you to point out the obvious?'

'No, I wanted to…to apologise.'

The way he said it made her think that wasn't the real reason she was there. She thought about Caitlyn's words, thought about her own reservations, and *knew* he didn't only want to apologise.

'I shouldn't have ambushed you this morning. I just… I didn't know what to do when they started asking questions about you.'

'*And* you thought having me on camera with you could only help your aim to buy the club.'

'Yes.'

He was watching her closely and she shifted.

'But that doesn't mean I don't feel bad about it.'

'*Do* you?'

'I do.'

'At least you're being honest.' And sincere, she thought, looking at his face.

'I'm sorry if I upset you.'

The words seemed more genuine now.

'I also wanted to thank you.'

He took a step forward, and instinct had her moving back. Then, because she didn't want it to seem as if she was afraid of being close to him—he *didn't* affect her that much, she assured herself—she stepped out onto the balcony.

The fresh air immediately eased some of the tension in her chest.

'Why do you want to thank me?' she asked when she heard him step out beside her.

'Our interview has gone viral.'

Ah, there it was. The real reason she was there.

'Yes, I've heard,' she said dryly. 'So you're saying thank you because we're all over social media?'

She could feel him watching her, and her heart hammered.

'Yes,' he answered, leaning against the railing as he'd done the night before at Nathan's. 'But more because the comments people have made are positive. My PR firm is very happy.' He paused. 'People really like you, Lily. And because of that they're starting to really like *me* again, too.'

She almost laughed. 'I'm glad it's working out for you.'

'You don't believe that people like you?'

'It doesn't matter what I believe.' But he was right. 'You got what you wanted.'

Jacques pushed himself up, his face revealing no emotion. 'Why don't you just say what you really want to say, Lily? Say what you mean.'

She looked at him. 'You used me.'

'*You* were the one who showed up at the studio today.' His voice was low. 'I didn't ask you to. In fact I'm pretty sure I remember telling you that you weren't the right person for it.'

His words sent a jolt through her.

'I know that. And I realise now that it was a mistake.'

She forced herself to calm the anxiety pumping

through her at the confrontation, told herself she was doing the right thing.

'But I showed up there because I chose to—which means I actually had a say. You took that away from me when you called me on to *live television* without checking with me first.'

A flash of regret crossed his face, but Lily refused to be swayed by it. She might as well say everything she needed to now.

'I would have never agreed to that if you'd asked me, and in my book that means you used me.'

The regret was gone from his face now, replaced by a stormy expression that she might have been wary of if she hadn't expected it.

But instead of the fire she knew he was capable of, he simply said, 'You knew what this would entail when you agreed to do it.'

She waited for more, but there was nothing. She shook her head.

'Why can't you just say that you shouldn't have done it? And then you can apologise sincerely—not because what you did *upset* me, but because you did it at all.'

He still didn't reply.

'I know the real reason you wanted to talk is because you need me,' she said. 'And because I'm already in two minds about helping you, it would probably be best if you stop with the silent treatment.'

CHAPTER NINE

THERE WAS A part of him that appreciated her temper. It was so different from the insecurity he could sense just beneath the surface, and the honesty was refreshing. But a bigger part of him was disturbed that Lily's words were describing his father.

Again.

From the moment he'd met her he'd been treating Lily as his father had treated his mother. Manipulating her, using her. But, unlike his mother, Lily had called him out on it both times. She wasn't as similar to the woman who'd raised him as he'd thought, Jacques realised. But did that matter when *he* was acting like his father? Someone he'd fought all his life *not* to become?

'I'm sorry I used you.'

'Thank you,' she answered softly, and he had to take a moment to compose himself. To protect himself against the emotions—the memories—he'd always managed to keep far, far away from his daily life.

Until he'd met Lily.

'So, will you help me now?' he asked when he was sure he had control of himself again.

'If we're being honest, I really don't want to.'

She looked at him, and his heart ached at the vulnerability he saw on her face.

'So I apologised for nothing?'

'No, you apologised because you want to be a decent human being.' She shot him a look that had him smiling and shook her head. 'You were kidding. Okay, well… A sense of humour.'

She shook her head again, and looked out to the beach.

'When you get over your surprise, how about you tell me what's going on?'

'I told you—I made a mistake this morning. And now I realise how big.'

'Because people are recognising you?'

'Yes, but more than that, too.'

She angled her shoulders so that he couldn't see her face. Again, his heart pulsed for her.

'My parents called this morning. They wanted to know why I hadn't told them we were dating.'

She turned back to him now, and his heart's reaction became harder to ignore.

'What did you say to them?' he asked, to distract himself.

'I lied.' She shrugged. 'What *could* I tell them? That I was pretending to be your girlfriend for a business deal? They would be so disappointed in me. And I've disappointed them enough.'

The words to ask how were at the tip of his tongue, but he stopped himself. He didn't want to become more invested in this woman. Not if he could help it.

'We're in this now, aren't we?' She looked up at him. 'We have to keep this going until the deal's done. Until people lose interest.'

Since it was exactly what he'd wanted, he thought he should confirm it to her with excitement. But instead, he found himself saying softly, 'Yeah, we do.'

She crossed her arms, sucking in her bottom lip in

such a defeated way that he couldn't help it when his words came tumbling out.

'Why did you do it? I'm not talking about the reason you already gave me.' He brushed off the explanation he knew she had ready. 'Sure, maybe you *did* come through this morning because you wanted to thank me or pay off a debt. But that wasn't the only reason.'

She tightened her arms around herself, and he knew he'd been right.

'You're *invested* in this somehow.'

Her face paled, but barely so. If he hadn't been so enthralled by the colour of her skin, by the features of her face that were so effortlessly breathtaking, he wouldn't have noticed.

Stop.

'No, I'm not.'

'Yes, you are.'

'If there *was* another reason, Jacques, why would I share it with you?'

She had straightened her spine, and he felt satisfaction pour through him. *This* Lily he could handle.

'So there *is* another reason?'

'Oh, for goodness' sake.' She threw her hands up, and then put them on her hips. 'If I tell you, you'll just use it as leverage to force me to keep the game going.'

Guilt burned in his stomach, but *that* he could easily ignore.

'You were the one who said that we have to go through with this. And telling me might remind you why you decided to do it in the first place. It might even give you the motivation you seem to need.'

Her eyes fluttered up to his, and he felt a punch in his gut at the emotion there. At the fire that sparked between them for the briefest moment.

Her hands fell from her sides—defeat, he thought—and her expression softened. And something gleamed in her eyes that made the voice in his head which was so concerned about his feelings when it came to Lily shout all the louder.

'What do you see out there?' she asked, gesturing to the beach.

He frowned. 'People?'

'Exactly. It's a Friday evening. People are going home from work after a hard week. They come to the beach to relax, enjoy a cocktail. Maybe read a book and unwind. And yet here *I* am with you.'

It took him a moment, but he got there.

'Your shop…?'

'Should be open—yes. I should be using the opportunity. Capitalising on it.' She paused. 'I used to. For a few months. But then keeping the store open at night took more money than I had.'

He waited for the rest, though he'd begun to put two and two together.

'I *was* at the studio this morning because I owed you. But I was also there because of that.'

She looked at him with a quiet strength he wondered if she knew she had.

'I've put more into this place than you could possibly imagine. I've sacrificed so much.'

She took a deep breath.

'My store is failing, Jacques,' she said in a voice that broke, and the expression on her face told him she thought *she* was failing, too. 'I'm barely staying afloat being open during the day. If I don't get more customers I won't be able to afford to pay the rent, or the electricity bill, or the rates. Not to mention pay my two staff members and the millions of other things small business owners need to pay.'

She shook her head, looked him in the eye, and he saw the fatigue. But then she straightened her shoulders again.

'So I thought if you mentioned my name, my occupation, it would drive more people into the store during the day, which might let me pay for keeping the store opening during the evening. I thought pretending to be your girlfriend would help my business.'

'So you were using *me*, too?'

'No!' she said sharply. 'I didn't trick you into doing anything you didn't want to. *You* were the one who wanted me there, and I saw how that might benefit the place I love so much. But I would never have done what you did to me.'

He knew he shouldn't have said those words the moment they'd left his lips, but he hadn't been able to help it. And now he wondered why he couldn't just let it go. Why he couldn't admit he'd been wrong.

'You didn't tell me any of that before I did the interview. *You* didn't even mention it when you were on TV.'

'I know.' She sighed. 'I didn't think it through properly. If you hadn't gone to get coffee I would have probably realised that and gone home before I embarrassed myself. And then I was on TV and I couldn't think straight. It was like a nightmare come true.'

'But you managed to defend me so well that people are saying I'm lucky to have you.'

'That's why I was there.'

Suddenly he remembered how struck he'd been when he'd seen her just before the interview. And how much what she'd said during the interview had meant to him. There was something about Lily—about the two of them together—that took Jacques completely out of his comfort zone.

And into a zone that forced him to *feel*.

'I don't always make the best decisions.'

Her words dragged him out of his thoughts. 'I'm glad you made this one.'

'I don't know if I can say the same,' she admitted softly.

'Well, you made the decision.' He stepped closer to her. 'And you were more prepared than I was when you did. Reading up on me, however creepy, shows me your decision wasn't entirely rash.'

Her lips curved, and the tension in his shoulders slackened.

'The things you said...they really helped. No one has ever said something like that about me.' Her eyes fluttered up at him and he quickly added, 'Not in public, I mean.'

'Yeah, I figured that when people kept asking me, "Is Jacques really the way you said he was on TV?" Mostly girls with hearts in their eyes, but it's something.'

'So you had more people in your store today?'

She sighed, gave him a look that told him she knew what he was doing.

'Yes.'

'It can keep being like this, Lily.'

'Yes, I *know* if I pretend to be your girlfriend some more my store will be a lot busier,' she said flatly. 'I know I don't really have a choice, Jacques. You don't have to keep trying to convince me.'

'Thanks for the confirmation. But I thought... Well, I was thinking about more than that.'

He wasn't sure why he'd faltered when his idea was actually a good one.

'I can help you use the momentum of this publicity to get regular customers. I can help with your business plan, with the accounts—with pretty much everything your shop needs to stay successful when this is all over. I can even give you a loan—'

He broke off when she stepped back abruptly.

'I don't want your money, Jacques. You can't *pay* me to do what you want me to.'

CHAPTER TEN

'I'M NOT PAYING YOU,' Jacques answered with a frown. 'I'm just offering you a loan to help get you on your feet again.'

'And would you have offered me that loan if you didn't need my help?'

Her breathing was much too rapid, and she forced herself to inhale and exhale slowly.

'No, I suppose not. But—'

'Then don't do it now,' she snapped, and turned away from him so that he couldn't see the tears in her eyes.

She suddenly felt incredibly tired. The interview, the store, the public, and now this conversation... She'd told him things she hadn't intended to because—well, because he'd *listened*. Maybe he even cared.

But that was just an illusion, she thought, and *she* was the magician, weaving a world where she believed in things that didn't exist. Like someone who was genuinely interested in her worries, her cares.

And his offer of money... It reminded her entirely too much of the way her relationship with Kyle had ended. If she accepted money from Jacques, as she had from the Van der Rosses, all the regret she'd felt since then would have been a lie. She would have been lying to *herself.* It would make her just as bad as she already thought she was for taking that money in the first place…

'I'm sorry, Lily, I didn't mean to offend you.'

'No, *I'm* sorry. I shouldn't have…' She took a breath. 'It's just been…so lonely. Who'd have thought starting a store would be lonely?'

She'd meant it as a joke, and was horrified when her eyes burned. Because it *had* been lonely. And carrying the burden of the store's fate alone…

She couldn't turn to her parents—they'd just say *I told you so* and try to make her see where she'd gone wrong. Because in their minds *she* would be the one in the wrong.

As she always was.

When she had complained about being bullied at school they'd asked her what *she* had done. When she'd broken off her engagement they'd asked her what *she* had done.

There was constant disapproval from them. A constant expectation of failure. Especially when the things she wanted were so different from what *they* wanted.

'I don't want your money, Jacques. But I *will* accept your help with my business skills. I want you to train me, show me where I'm going wrong. But that's all.' She paused, watched his face for his agreement. When she saw it there she nodded in response.

'Is the money thing…? Is it because of Kyle?'

Her insides felt as if they'd been dipped into an ice bucket. 'What?'

'He had money. I thought maybe you didn't want to be reminded of it.'

The ice defrosted, but her body still shook.

'You're right. I don't want to be. I just want that part of my life to be over.'

He was quiet for a moment, and then he said, 'It's been bothering me for a while. You and him together.'

His face was clear while he spoke, but something in his eyes made her belly warm.

'I can't see it.'

'Because he's rich and handsome and successful and I'm just okay-looking with a struggling store?'

'Stop that,' he commanded. 'I don't want to hear you talk about yourself like that any more. And I sure as hell don't want to hear you make him sound like he's some kind of prize.'

She felt a flush stain her cheeks. 'I'm sorry.'

'And stop apologising. You have nothing to apologise for.'

He walked towards her, and her heart sped with each step he took.

'I'm going to say this once, because you need to hear it.'

He lifted her chin with a finger, forcing her to look into his eyes.

'You are the most...*captivating* woman I have ever met. Your hair makes me want to slide my fingers through it so I can see the curls bounce back.' He pulled at one, as if to illustrate his words. 'Sometimes when I look into your eyes I feel like you're looking through me. And that doesn't scare me—even though it absolutely should. And those lips...'

He brushed his thumb over them, making her tremble.

'They make me regret stopping last night. Every time I see them I want to taste them again, to check whether they're really as sweet as I remember.' He lifted his eyes to hers. 'Don't tell me you're "okay-looking" when you have that effect on me. When I have eyes, Lily.'

There was a pause while she tried to catch her breath.

'We have an audience.'

His fingers grazed her chin again, tightened slightly when she tried to turn her head to look at what—who— he was talking about.

'This won't look nearly as genuine if you check to see where the cameras are,' he murmured, tucking a curl behind her ear and moving so that there was no more space between them.

Any hope she had of catching her breath again disappeared. Not because of the cameras—though somewhere at the back of her mind she *was* worried about being photographed after a hard day's work. No, that didn't bother her as much when she was still recovering from the seduction of his words. From the proximity of his body.

The fresh, manly smell of his cologne filled her lungs. The easy way he touched her made her see only him, hear only him. She wanted to shake her head clear, to beg the logical part of her mind to take control again.

But all her senses were completely captivated by him.

His hand wrapped around her waist, lightly at first, and before she knew it she was pressed against his body.

'Is this what our arrangement is going to look like?' she managed to ask, and his eyes darkened.

'I really hope so...'

It was as if he had no control over his body, and his lips had touched hers before he had finished speaking.

She *did* taste as sweet as he remembered, and it made every regret he knew he'd have when he could think again worth it. He fought against the heat that demanded passion and slowly explored her mouth, relishing every feeling, every thrill that went through his body.

His hands made their way up over the back of her waist, loving how the curves of her body felt under his touch. Loving the quiver that it sent through Lily's body. His right hand moved further along, brushing the side of her breast and making them both shudder. The sane part of him—the one that reminded him they were being watched—was the only thing that kept his hand from lingering there, and it finally made its way to its intended destination.

He slid his hand through her curls and tilted her head to give him better access to her neck, pulling his lips from hers so that they could memorise the feel of her pulse against them. The moan that he heard in return made him abandon his resolve to take it slowly, and when he took her mouth this time their kiss was more passionate, more dangerous.

He would never have his fill of her, he thought, and his hands gripped her hips to pull her even tighter towards him.

The shock of desire his action brought made him break away, and he took a step back, fighting to control his body. And when that didn't entirely work he just wanted to control his lungs.

'You are...'

Lily looked rumpled and it made him feel better when he saw the way her chest heaved just as his did.

'Dangerous, Jacques. You make me...'

She didn't continue her sentence, but her words helped sober him from the drunkenness of passion.

'Feel?' he finished for her. 'I make you feel, don't I?'

Her shake of the head didn't matter when he knew it was the truth. She did the same thing to him.

'I'm sure we've given those watching more than enough to talk about,' she said, instead of answering him, looking at the small crowd that had gathered behind the fence around his property. 'How did they even know we were here?'

'We're standing on a balcony, Lily,' he replied dryly. 'And we were talking for the better part of an hour. It wouldn't take much for people on the very busy beach to notice us.'

'Okay, fine. Let's go back inside, then.'

They walked back into his flat, and he closed the door so their audience would lose interest.

And then he watched her gather herself, and found he was utterly taken by her.

By the simple green dress she wore that flared out at her waist. By the hair that was tied to the top of her head in a bun, curls spiralling out wherever they could manage it.

She didn't look like any other woman he knew, he thought. And *damn* but she drew him in like no other woman ever had.

'Would you like to have dinner with me?'

'No, no, no,' Lily said quickly. 'There is no part of me that wants to do that after that kiss.'

'It was just pretend, Lily. It wasn't real.'

'I'm not interested in trying to convince you that you're fooling yourself if you want to believe that. But I *will* say that we need to draw a line if I agree to go through with this.'

'I thought you'd already agreed?'

'I can change my mind.'

She watched him for a moment, and Jacques wondered how now, during the most important deal of his life, he'd found the only woman who stood up to him.

'Look, I'm not going to pretend like there isn't an attraction between us, because clearly...' She waved a hand between them and his lips curved. 'But I don't want to pursue it. And I don't want you to either.'

The seriousness of her tone faded the remnants of his smile, and for the first time he heard the plea in her voice.

'Those are my conditions,' she said after a pause, and when she looked at him his heart stuttered at the confirmation of her plea. And although there was a part of him that wanted to tell her he couldn't accept those conditions, he nodded.

'That's fair.'

'So you agree?' she asked, eyebrows raised. 'Anything that happens between us from now on is strictly business. We can't complicate things by letting pleasure cloud our judgement.'

He was surprised by how much he didn't want to agree with her, but he nodded.

'If that's what you want, yes, I agree.'

'It is what I want,' she confirmed, though her tone made him think she wasn't as convinced as she wanted to be. 'Then I will have dinner with you. Because you're not calling me on to live television again just because you don't know enough about me.'

'That's why I suggested it.'

At least it should have been.

'Could I just have a moment to freshen up?'

'Sure.'

He showed her to the bathroom, and then tried to gather his thoughts. He needed to focus on his task. It hadn't left his mind once in the few months that he'd been trying to secure the sale, and yet with Lily he constantly needed to remind himself of it.

It was just too easy to get caught up in getting to know her. In wondering how she could afford prime retail property with modern and expensive décor on Big Bay Beach in Cape Town when she didn't have the money to sustain her store. She must have got the initial money *somewhere*. And after her reaction to his offer of a loan he thought it had to be connected.

And then there was her plea to keep things professional. After the way she'd dodged his question about Kyle, Jacques knew he was the reason why she'd asked.

Maybe he would have reacted the same way if his fiancée had cheated on him. But he'd never had a relationship last long enough for him to know what being in one felt like. He'd never wanted to be responsible for another woman's feelings. He'd had a lifetime's worth growing up with his mother. It was just a bonus that avoiding relationships meant he never needed to worry about how much of his father he had in him. About whether he was as cold, as oblivious to his partner's feelings.

And since Lily now had him suspecting that there was a little *too* much of his father in him, it was for the best that he just focus on business. On the deal that would help him make peace with his past.

He'd made progress. The TV interview that morning had had an incredibly positive influence on his image. But he didn't know if it was enough. So he would spend more time with Lily, and then hopefully Jade and Riley would tell him his reputation had been restored and the sponsors had changed their minds.

And if they hadn't...

You'd marry her?

His gut turned at the thought, and the strength of his resistance stunned him. There was immediate panic because of it, and he forced himself to breathe. Told himself it was only because marrying her would go against what they'd agreed on. It had nothing to do with the fact that marrying her would definitely be manipulative, knowing what he knew now. Their attraction. Her vulnerability. The protectiveness she inspired in him...

He turned when he felt a hand on his back, his heart thudding at his thoughts.

'Are you ready?'

'Yeah,' he answered, and cleared his throat when he heard the rasp of his voice. 'There are still a few people outside, though, so maybe we should stay here. I'll pour some wine.'

He wasn't suggesting it because he needed to compose himself. And he wasn't heading to where he kept his alcohol because he needed it to help him do that.

If he needed to marry Lily, he would. It was business, after all. But because of their agreement he'd talk to her first. That was fair, wasn't it? And it wouldn't be manipulative then, would it?

It made him feel calmer, that decision—until a voice asked him what had changed. He hadn't liked it when Riley and Jade had suggested marriage, but he'd believed he would have done it if he'd had to. And definitely without reservations over *who* he was marrying.

So the question wasn't *what* had changed, but who had changed *him*.

And really, he thought as he looked at Lily, should he even bother answering that question?

CHAPTER ELEVEN

'YOUR FLAT IS LOVELY, by the way,' Lily said to break the tension.

Tension she'd thought had started to subside before she'd freshened up.

'Thank you. Though I don't know if I should believe you, based on your tone.'

Something in *his* tone told her something had changed. But she was determined to keep things civil between them, and she wasn't sure if she could if she asked him about it.

'It really is lovely,' she insisted, settling on the safe subject. 'It just doesn't feel like you live here.'

'Why not?'

'You don't have a table on your balcony,' she said, and her pulse picked up—just a little—at the attention he aimed at her. 'That would have been the first thing I would have done when I moved in. I would eat my breakfast there, my lunch... Actually, I'd probably use any opportunity I could to appreciate that view.'

'I can appreciate the view fine from here,' he responded in a low tone.

She turned, saw that he was looking at her, and blushed. 'We had an agreement.'

'We still have the agreement. But I don't think it would

do any harm to flirt.' He grinned, but something felt off. As if he was saying the words on autopilot.

'Maybe not for you,' she said, and then closed her eyes. She hadn't meant for that to come out.

She held her breath, waiting for him to respond, and then sighed when he just said, 'You're right, though, I don't live here.'

She turned back at the proximity of his voice, took the glass of wine he handed her.

'Where *do* you live, then?'

'Near the office. I spend more time there than at home anyway.'

'Because you have nothing to go home to?'

There was a pause. 'Maybe.'

He gestured for her to take a seat, and she did, nearly groaning when the couch enveloped her aching body. It reminded her that she should be at home, soaking in a bath and drinking a glass of wine *there* instead of with Jacques.

She realised then that he hadn't really answered her question. It *had* been a little invasive, she considered. But it had fallen so freely from her lips because it was true in her own case. When she was at home her mind had nothing else to do but think about how she had failed in her life. How her parents had been right…how she should have never thought she was good enough to run a successful store. How running a business required business acumen, not the creative mind *she* had.

And when it was done with that her mind would start on how she should have just left Kyle without a backward glance, instead of accepting money so that she felt as if she'd paid with her soul.

'Maybe we should start with something a little…

less...' she suggested when her thoughts made her chest tighten.

'I think that would be for the best,' he answered, and sipped from his wine glass. 'Tell me about your family.'

It was an innocent question, but she felt a wall go up around her heart. She had to tell him *something*, though.

'There's nothing out of the ordinary there,' she said slowly. 'My mom used to be a paediatrician. She's retired now, but she still helps out at the local hospital three days a week. My dad's a couple of years younger than her, so he's still working. He's an engineer.'

'What kind?'

She tilted her head, a smile tickling her lips that he'd thought to ask.

'Civil.'

He nodded. 'Siblings?'

'None. I'm the only child.'

He frowned. 'It doesn't sound like you're happy about that.'

She'd heard that, too. The slight dip in her voice that had tainted her words. But what could she tell him? That her parents, with their engineering and medical degrees and professional stability, had expected her to follow in their footsteps from a young age? That when she'd proved to be different from them they hadn't been able to adjust? That instead they'd just tried to apply to her the mould they were used to and hadn't seen how it had eroded her confidence, her self-worth?

'No,' she answered him. 'My parents have...' She stopped herself, and cleared her throat. 'It's nothing.'

A single raised eyebrow sent her heart jumping.

'It's something.' There was a pause. 'Lily?'

His tone was a mixture of forced patience and genuine curiosity, and she knew if she were talking about anything else it would have made her smile. Now, she chose her words carefully.

'They just…their expectations of me are a bit high.'

'Why?'

She lifted her eyes at the softness his voice had now, felt the warmth in his gaze right down to her toes.

'They're very…rigid. Things are straightforward for them. Simple. Do you want to be a doctor? Study for a medical degree. Engineer? Study engineering.' They were simple examples, but she saw that he understood what she meant. 'I'm not straightforward.'

'And they can't understand that.'

'No, they can't.'

'I understand not living up to your parents' expectations.'

She looked up to see Jacques staring out at the beach. When he looked back at her she once again saw that stormy expression in his eyes.

'But the more important question is whether you've lived up to your expectations of *yourself*?'

She'd never thought about it, she realised in surprise. *Had* she lived up to her own expectations? Did she even *have* expectations of herself? Her mind scrambled for an answer and she bit her lip. She had goals and dreams. Why were they so difficult to remember now?

Because they're so closely tied to other people's expectations of you.

She frowned. Was her store failing because her parents had expected it to so she did too? Did she believe that she could do better, that she could *be* better, because that was what Kyle had expected of her? What did the money she'd accepted from Kyle's family—the first decision she'd ever made for herself—say about her expectations of herself? What did it *make* her?

'Have *you*?' she asked, desperate when she looked at Jacques and realised he saw too much. 'Lived up to your own expectations?'

Though his expression gave nothing away, she saw the hand holding his glass of wine tighten, and she realised the answer was no.

It made her feel better—a little less vulnerable—and because it did she said, 'Fortunately no one will be asking us that question.'

She nodded at the relief she saw in his eyes.

'But they might expect you to know that my parents live about an hour away from here, in Langebaan. And they'll expect me to know about *your* family. I already know Nathan. How about you tell me about your parents? Other than their ridiculous expectations of you, of course.'

She'd said it lightly, but his face hardened, a light going out in it.

'Neither of my parents work. They have money—a lot of it—that my grandfather made in the mining business. They keep busy, of course, but they don't have jobs.'

'Oh,' she said slowly, processing this new information.

It reminded her that Nathan worked for the Van der Rosses not only because he was a good lawyer, but because he had the connections to get into the biggest law firm in the Western Cape. It made his humility, his good nature, so much more appealing.

'Where do they live?'

'Somerset West.'

'And since you live on the opposite side of Cape Town that puts a nice distance between you and your parents,' she said, and saw confirmation in his eyes before something else eclipsed it...guilt? Because she thought it was, she added, 'I'm not judging. It's the same with my parents.'

'Distance helps. You don't have to constantly be reminded of how you've fallen short.'

He understood, she thought.

'Not that it matters in my case, since I haven't seen them in seven years.'

'*Seven* years?' He nodded, but didn't meet her eyes. 'That's when...'

'When I destroyed my career?'

Now he looked at her. 'Yes.'

The admission was difficult for him, she saw, and felt a little relief at that. They were on the same page, then, sharing difficult things with each other. She still worried that she had told him too much. But it felt good finally to admit that she couldn't be what her parents wanted her to be. It felt good finally to talk to someone who understood. Caitlyn didn't, and since she was Lily's only friend there hadn't been any other options.

Now there was Jacques.

She didn't quite know how to feel about that. So she settled on something a little more familiar.

'So, how about we get to that dinner you promised me?'

Jacques's lips curved into a smile. It broke some of the tension he felt about his surprising admission. The tension that had started when he'd realised she was changing him.

And he'd only known her for two days.

'I usually have my housekeeper prepare meals for me when I know I'll be staying here,' he said, and took her wine glass from her as she tried to get out of the hole the couch had created for her body.

He'd bought the piece of furniture specifically because it had that ability, which felt like heaven after a tough rugby practice or match. But watching her struggle now gave him a new appreciation for it. Her cheeks were flushed as she tried to scoot her way to the edge of the seat. Though it helped to get her feet closer to the ground, it made her dress ride up, exposing her thighs.

A ball of fire dropped in his stomach, turning his amusement into something more serious. Something more dangerous. It rooted his feet to the ground even as it woke every nerve in his body. She hadn't noticed this new development, and the more she moved the higher the dress went.

Eventually she sighed and, without looking at him, lifted a hand for his assistance.

It took him a moment to move—to force his body to behave—and then he set their wine glasses on the table and quickly took her hand, pulling her up without paying attention to the force he used. Though it helped her out of the seat, it also made her lose her balance—and before he could totally comprehend what had happened she had fallen against his chest.

His arms went around her, steadying her, but when she looked up at him, the colour of her skin still tinged with pink, rational thought flew out of his mind. Their eyes met, and the heat that always simmered between them turned into a boil. His arms tightened, pulling her closer to his body. Her curves fitted perfectly there, he thought, and the air in his lungs thickened. Her eyes had widened, but she hadn't protested at their proximity. Instead her arms had wound around his neck, and those full lips of hers had parted.

He remembered their taste from that afternoon, when he'd kissed her for what he'd told her was the public's sake. But it had really been because he'd had to know whether the attraction, the pull he felt for her was real. And now that he knew it was—now that he could acknowledge that despite all his playboy-like dating years he'd never wanted another woman as intensely as he wanted Lily—he wondered how their kiss would be.

Whether now that they were in his flat, away from the public, their kiss would turn into something more. Something that would sate the nagging need he felt for her...

'Jacques!' She interrupted his thoughts in a hoarse voice. 'You...*we*...we promised.'

Somewhere at the back of his mind it bothered him that she'd had to remind him—*again*—of that promise, that agreement they'd made only a few moments earlier. It seemed vague, faded—just like the goal that had consumed his mind from the moment he'd learned the Shadows Rugby Club was for sale.

The realisation made him step back, put some distance between them.

But still his body yearned.

'I'm sorry.'

'Me, too,' she answered, and something in her voice—her eyes—made him wonder if she was apologising because they had stopped things before they got...*interesting*.

There was a long pause, and then he heard her release a shaky breath. The sound revved him into action. 'So. Food?'

'Yeah—what do you have?'

He forced his mind to focus and picked up his wine, downing it even as he wished for something stronger.

'I didn't tell my housekeeper I was coming,' he said, only then realising that he didn't have much to offer her.

'I think there's some lasagne left over from when I was here last week.'

'Did you invite me to stay here for dinner without having dinner to offer me?'

Embarrassment stirred beneath the desire he'd felt just a few moments earlier.

'Yes. But to be fair I wasn't exactly expecting this. I thought we'd go out.'

'Do you have any ingredients to make something?'

He walked to the kitchen, checked in cupboards that held only cutlery, crockery and the few items he needed to make coffee.

'I'm afraid not.'

She stared at him for a while, and then a smile crept onto her lips.

'What?' he asked, as his mouth twitched to mirror hers.

She shrugged. 'It's just nice to know you don't think things through sometimes either. You know—like the rest of us normal people.'

He smiled at her, but her words had scratched at a wound he'd thought he had buried a long time ago. He'd always wanted to be *normal*. Normal children had normal families. Normal families had fathers who cared about their sons and didn't brush them aside for something—anything—better.

He pulled the fridge open with enough force that the door swung from his hand, hitting the counter and then his arm. Since there was nothing in it there was no damage, but he had to close his eyes to control his anger. To control *his* damage.

'I was only teasing,' Lily said from behind him, and he turned, his heart softening when he saw the uncertain look on her face.

'I know. I was just thinking that I should have something for you other than this.'

He gestured to the fridge. It held only a half-empty bottle of orange juice. It was a lame excuse, and they both knew it, but Lily didn't call him on it. Instead she watched him, the look of uncertainty fading, leaving only a shadow of vulnerability on her face.

He could see that vulnerability every time he looked at her, he realised. It was the reason he hadn't wanted her to take part in his plan in the first place. And it was the reason she was the *best* person to take part in his plan. She was *real*—with real feelings, real emotions.

She had the same concerns he did—that she had fallen short of the expectations her parents had of her. And while he was sure that was because she hadn't had the courage to tell her parents to adjust those expectations, his concerns were a result of years and years of trying but never succeeding.

Once he'd realised nothing he did would ever mean anything to Dale Brookes—would ever make his father *love* him—he had stopped trying. But he hadn't given up on his mother until the night of the championship game. He hadn't been able to believe that after everything Dale had put her through—after everything she'd seen the man put him and Nathan through—she'd stayed with him after he'd promised her for the umpteenth time that he would change.

Not even the taunts his father had aimed at him after his mother had decided not to leave had given her a clue that he wouldn't *ever* change. And after that night—after the subsequent events that had ruined his career—he had cut ties with his parents. He'd put away those protective instincts he'd felt for his mother. Had vowed never to apply them to another woman.

Except Lily.

'How about that lasagne?'

She interrupted his thoughts and he frowned as he tried to remember what they were talking about.

'Let me check.' He checked the freezer, saw there was nothing in it, and closed it again. 'I'm sure there aren't any people outside any more. We should go out.'

'Because there's no food in your freezer?'

'Are you mocking my hosting abilities?'

'Who? Me?' She fluttered her eyelashes. 'I would *never* do that to my oh-so-gracious host.'

He eased with the banter. 'What do you feel like eating?'

'What's the closest place?'

He frowned. 'It doesn't have to be close. We can drive somewhere nice—'

'No.' She cleared her throat and pulled the jersey she still wore tightly around herself again. 'Let's just get something at the closest place.'

It took a moment for him to put all the pieces together.

'You don't *want* us to be seen in public?' When she looked away, he shook his head. 'Lily, that's not a realistic expectation for this whole plan. We're—'

'Just not tonight, okay?'

It was a plea that went straight to his heart.

'I've given people enough of me today. And I look fa—' She stopped, looked at him with uncertainty and then finished, 'I look frumpy in this dress.'

'No, you don't,' he said immediately. 'And you weren't going to say that.'

'What?'

But she'd walked into the living room, away from him, and he realised she knew exactly what he was talking about.

'Yesterday you said you were too heavy for me to lift you.' He was talking to himself mostly, but when he saw her face he knew his gut had been right. 'Lily, were you going to say *fat*?'

CHAPTER TWELVE

'NO,' SHE ANSWERED QUICKLY. 'Of course not.'

'Why on earth would you think that?' he asked her, dismissing the obvious lie.

She wanted to be flattered by the incredulous tone he used, but her embarrassment was too much for her to think of anything else.

'We should probably get going.'

Please don't push, she thought, and while the minutes passed repeated the plea in her mind.

'There's a place we can walk to from here. It's secluded...intimate. Something only the residents around here know about.'

Relief pummelled the reply from her mouth. 'Yes, that sounds perfect.'

He nodded. 'We can go down there.' He gestured to the balcony stairs.

She followed him down the steps, through the gate he'd opened in the fence that no longer had to keep out a crowd. Her feet felt heavier with each stride. It didn't take long for her to realise the weight had nothing to do with the sand they were walking on, but guilt.

Guilt for avoiding his question. For lying to him. She didn't *want* to tell him, but she felt compelled to and she wasn't sure why. Though she wanted to ignore it, his silence made her feel as if he was pulling back. It sent waves of panic through her that soon took control of her tongue.

'I was overweight for a very long time.' Her insides shrivelled at the words, but she knew it was too late to stop. 'I lost some weight when I started university, and then a little more while I studied. It was hard.' She cleared her throat when her voice suddenly went hoarse. 'I've been struggling to keep it off since then.'

He didn't respond, but gripped her hand. The warmth from it spread through her body.

'You still feel like you're overweight?'

'I...' She took a deep breath and was grateful for the slight pressure from his hand. 'I'm not perfect. I'll never be a supermodel.'

'And in your mind that means you're fat?'

She flinched at the word, just as she had the first time he'd used it. But it was her own fault. She'd thought it first—had almost said it—and she couldn't shy away from it now because it offended her But it brought back such memories—hurtful ones that made her want to fade into the background.

Before she could respond, he stopped, and put a hand around her waist, pulling her in to his side.

'We're here.'

She'd been so lost in thought, so lost in the difficulty of their conversation, that she hadn't seen the beach torches that led to a small wooden deck. The deck seated four tables of two and four, then led into a beach cottage that had been renovated into a restaurant. Paraffin lamps lit the deck, lining the two steps that led up to it and the wooden banister that surrounded it.

Jacques's hand still held hers as they walked up the steps and she saw the beach-themed green and blue interior of the restaurant. A stocky young man greeted Jacques with enthusiasm, with recognition, and seated them at the only free table on the deck.

'This is… Wow, it's beautiful.' She looked out to where the moon lit the sea, and only then saw the small dance floor just beyond the deck. 'Do people actually *use* that?'

He shrugged. 'I've never actually been here to see that.'

'But you *have* been here before. With other women, of course, considering the waiter is now discussing you with his friend over there.'

She nodded her head to where the man was animatedly speaking to another waiter, gesturing in their direction.

'He might just be a fan of mine.'

'He might be,' she agreed. 'But since the other waiter just sent me a knowing glance I suspect I'm right.'

He smiled, but didn't meet her eyes. 'You are.'

Though she wasn't surprised, she *was* a little annoyed—too much for someone who supposedly didn't care about Jacques's past.

And then he said, 'But you're the first I've brought here at night.'

'And that's important because…?'

'Because night-time dates set the tone for the rest of the evening. This kind of place…it's intimate.'

Her heart pounded at the implication.

'And the waiter you pointed out just took a picture of us. He'll probably post it to all his social networks.'

That's more realistic than thinking he wants to be intimate with you, Lily.

'So "secluded" and "intimate" don't necessarily mean private?'

'We aren't supposed to be private, Lily,' he reminded

her. 'But I can ask him not to post it. To delete the picture, even. I doubt his boss would want him taking pictures of the restaurant's patrons anyway.'

'You'd do that? For me?'

He didn't meet her eyes. 'For both of us. We still have a month until the club's sale is finalised, and I think we've had enough exposure for today.'

But she knew he'd just given her that reason because he couldn't admit he *would have* done it for her. It had her insides glowing.

'It's fine—let him post it. What harm could it possibly do after all we've already done today?'

He nodded his thanks, and then called the waiter over to order wine.

It gave her time to think about why his words had warmed her so much. They shared an attraction, yes. And if she hadn't lived the kind of life she had perhaps that would mean something. But attraction didn't last. Reality would soon catch up with them—just as it had with her and Kyle. And Jacques would soon realise—just as Kyle had—that Lily simply wasn't enough.

She'd thought about it a lot after she'd broken off their engagement.

Lily knew she would have made Kyle a decent wife. She'd passed her degree—a Bachelor of *Arts*, much to her parents' chagrin—at one of the top universities in the country, so she'd have been able to engage with his peers without embarrassing him. She had lost weight, so she'd looked fine, she supposed, but not good enough that she'd threaten any of the supermodel wives of the business acquaintances Kyle would have to charm. And she had been easily manipulated—which had probably been a huge part of her appeal. Easily bullied.

Lily would have done almost anything Kyle had asked because—well, because he'd asked her.

She could remember the times when she hadn't responded favourably and had had him pressuring her. She'd given in so quickly, terrified he would leave if she didn't. And yet despite all that Lily had clearly still lacked *something*. And that something had been significant enough that Kyle had turned to another woman to get it.

No, she thought again. Jacques's interest in her wouldn't last for very long. Not once he found out she wasn't anything more than a prop in his charade.

But she could enjoy the present. She could enjoy the fact that she was in a restaurant—a beautiful one she would never have discovered otherwise—with a man she liked. And, being in the present, Lily didn't have to think about the context that word 'liked' was being used.

'You're perfect, you know,' he said when the waiter had left, so sincerely that she regretted that he wouldn't want her soon. 'Your body, your weight... You don't have to worry about it.'

'Thank you,' she said softly. And then, because the way he was looking at her gave her gooseflesh, she continued, 'Like I said, I've lost a lot of weight. Now I try to keep what I eat appropriate, so that I don't gain it again.'

'That isn't the only thing you do.' Jacques's voice was low. 'You wear clothes you think hide your body. And even then you pull at them so they don't cling where they aren't supposed to.'

He paused when the waiter arrived to pour their wine. As soon as he was gone, Jacques continued.

'You worry about what people think about the way you look. So much so that you put a jersey on during a warm evening just in case someone sees you. Am I right?'

Her vocal cords wouldn't work. Not that there were any words for her to say after Jacques's little speech. It stunned her—shook her—that he was so perceptive. That he'd seen things she hadn't paid much attention to. She cringed that she hadn't been able to hide them. Felt the mortification balling in her stomach coated by anger.

'The judgement in your voice... Is that because you think I shouldn't care what people think?'

His brow furrowed. 'I wasn't *judging* you, Lily. But I do think you could worry a little less about it.'

'Because that's worked so well for *you*?'

It was a low blow—one she'd made deliberately, out of anger. But when she saw him recoil she immediately felt ashamed.

'I'm sorry. I shouldn't have said that.'

'But you were right.'

He shrugged, and she could almost see the weight that lay heavy on his shoulders. It made her feel even worse.

'No, *you* were right. I... I said that because I *know* you're right. And yet somehow... Well, some scars just don't go away.'

'Kyle?'

Again his perceptiveness was disturbing.

'Yes. But he was in a long line of others.'

'Then *why* did you date him, Lily?'

Because his tone was pleading with her, and because he was asking her for the second time—third, if she counted the night they'd met—she told him.

'He was interested in me. After years of no one wanting me, of feeling like I wasn't enough at home or at school, this successful, attractive man wanted *me*. So I ignored all the signs that told me he was just like the people who had bullied me in my childhood. It took catching him cheating to finally open my eyes.'

She didn't blame him for the silence that followed. But that didn't help her feel less exposed.

'I didn't realise...'

She lifted her glass to her lips, saw that her hands were shaking. 'Why would you?'

'I never liked him.'

He said it in a gruff voice, and it made her smile.

'You have good instincts.'

'And you blame yourself for *not* having them?'

Her fingers curled around the stem of the wine glass. 'No, I don't. My gut knew all along that he wasn't the right person for me. I just didn't listen.'

Because she'd already told him too much, she told herself there was no point in holding back now.

'I blame myself for believing that I couldn't do better.'

'But you know now that you can.'

It was a statement that told her he wouldn't accept any other.

'Yes.'

'Lily, you have to *mean* it.'

'I *do* mean it.'

'No, you don't. You may believe it in part, but something's keeping you from believing it fully.'

She felt a door slam shut in her heart.

'Let's order.'

CHAPTER THIRTEEN

IT TOOK JACQUES a moment to realise he'd been shut out. Another to deal with the rush of emotions that realisation brought. The anger was there, and the frustration. As was the curiosity. But the feeling that was strongest was the desire to make her *believe*. She didn't have to be defined by people's opinions. By one decision.

You're trying to convince yourself.

He shook it off. He didn't need to indulge thoughts that came from nowhere. But he *did* need to say something— this *one* thing—so that he wouldn't have to think about it over and over that night when they'd parted.

He waited for her to order, knowing she would use that as an excuse if he didn't, and placed his own. When the waiter had left, he said, 'You're a strong woman, Lily. Even if you don't believe it right now, some day you will and I'll have told you first.'

He'd wanted to reach out, to lay a hand over hers, but the look on her face had his hand sticking to his thigh. Her eyes were glossed with emotions that he felt in his own chest, her face a picture he didn't think he would ever be able to forget.

There was surprise, yes. But there was also hope. Pleasure, too. All because he had seen something in her that he now realised had been whittled away after years of being bullied.

What he wouldn't have given to see that look on his mother's face just once…

'Thank you.'

He nodded, unable to find words when his mind, his heart, were in turmoil.

'So, the flat…' She cleared her throat. 'Why did you buy it if you don't spend enough time there to have more than half a bottle of orange juice in your fridge?'

Grateful for the change in topic, he answered, 'I bought it after my first big rugby pay-cheque. The club is based down the road from here. It made sense to live close by. I could walk to and from the daily practices, and I was able to leave my car behind when we had away matches.'

'But you don't spend much time there now. So why do you still have the flat?'

'Because…because it reminds me of the happiest times of my life.'

There was another beat of silence, and then Lily said, 'That's why you want the club, too? Because it represents something good in your life?'

'Are we going to spend the whole evening talking about things that make us uncomfortable?'

He reached for his wine, drank it in one gulp. When he set it down he saw that she was watching him. She gave him a small, comforting smile.

'Seems like we can't get away from it.'

'We could if we just stopped now. If we talked about something innocuous like the weather.'

'It *is* a lovely evening,' she agreed, lifting her wine in a mock toast.

He smiled, then sobered. 'What do you want to know?'

His own words would have surprised him if he hadn't felt the shift that was happening between them. And, though he'd resisted it from the moment he'd first felt it, it still seemed to have power over him.

It still seemed to compel him.

'I want to know what really happened the night of that game,' she said, as he had known she would.

'I got into a fight, got a red card—my team lost and I got suspended.' It sounded crass, but it was the only way he could tell her.

'I know. I read all that in the papers. What I want to know is *why*?' she said softly. 'It's clear how much that time in your life meant to you. How much it *still* means to you. What could have happened to make you give it up?'

He took a deep breath, opened his mouth, and then shook his head.

He tried again. 'I told you my grandfather was in the mining business?'

She nodded.

'That was my mother's father. He spent years building his business, and the family name grew with it. By the time he retired he was a millionaire, with his name appearing on every rich or most successful list in South Africa.'

He paused and ran a hand through his hair.

'It meant people knew the family name—who they were. Here and overseas, since my grandfather had started trading abroad. If you aren't careful, having that kind of money and power tends to make people take advantage.' Another pause. 'My mother wasn't careful.'

He stopped, tension tight in every part of his body. He didn't look at her. He didn't want to see the empathy he knew would be there.

'She was an only child—my grandmother died during

childbirth—and my grandfather sent her overseas to live with his sister while she went to school.'

He took another breath.

'She got pregnant with me there. My grandfather was furious. She'd just finished school. With his connections, my mother would have had the world at her feet.'

He lifted his eyes to hers.

'He made it clear that she couldn't come back here. Not when she was unmarried and pregnant.'

She nodded, making him see she was familiar with the inflexible values of past generations.

'My mother decided to get married to spare my grandfather the embarrassment. It wasn't too bad for her, considering how much she loved my father. He just didn't love *her*.'

Anger still heated his blood at the thought.

'But he loved her money. There's no proof that he planned the whole thing, but I *know* he did.'

He could almost taste the bitterness on his tongue.

'We moved back to SA and my grandfather died a few years later. My mom had just fallen pregnant with Nathan, but my father's lack of interest in us become clear when my grandfather was no longer around. He didn't have to pretend to be a family man any more. My mother had inherited most of the money—the rest was in a trust fund for us—but since they were married her money was his, too.'

He shook his head when he realised he was saying too much.

'You didn't ask to know all this.'

'No,' she agreed. 'But since you've told me there must be a reason.'

He nodded, and tried to build up his nerve to tell her the rest.

'I watched my father treat my mother—and us—poorly for most of my life. I tried to get her to leave him, but she was clinging so hard to the memory of the man he had been when he was wooing her—when he was pretending to be someone he wasn't—that she wouldn't. Until she found out he'd been lying to her about the money he was spending. She could take his uninterest and harsh words, but lying about money was too much for her.'

He shook his head, still not quite believing that *that* had been more important to her than her children's well-being.

'I got her to consider making him leave, and on the night of the championship we packed his bags. We were kicking him out. But when he found out it didn't take long for his charm to soften my mother's defences. A few words, compliments, promises, and she took him back. Not even my begging was enough to make her reconsider.'

He felt Lily's hand over his, and looked down to see it was covering his clenched fist. He forced himself to uncurl it and took a deep breath. He wasn't done yet.

'He turned on me that night. Said things I don't want to remember but can't forget. No matter how much I try.'

He took another breath as the memories flew through his mind.

Failure. Disappointment. Useless.

'I wasn't fighting the opposing team that night, Lily...'

There was a beat of silence before she said what he couldn't bring himself to.

'You were fighting your father.'

Lily's heart broke when he nodded, and she entwined her fingers with his, squeezing. But the moment was inter-

rupted when the waiter brought their food, and she pulled
her hand away, grateful for the break in the tension.

A small wave of guilt flowed through her when she
looked at the burger in front of her, but since it was
accompanied by a salad—and she hadn't eaten since
lunch—she figured it was okay.

'Why did you never go back?'

'It was too late. I got suspended for three years—the
maximum for what I did. Even if a team had wanted me,
being out the game that long meant I wouldn't have had
the same skills.'

'I'm sorry.'

He shrugged. 'It doesn't matter now.'

'But it *does*,' she said, wondering why he was pretending it didn't after everything he'd told her. 'Isn't that why
you're doing this? Because of how much it means to you?'

She could see he was considering it, so she gave him
time and dug into her meal. The burger was juicy, soft,
and for the first time in a long time she found that she
was enjoying a meal without feeling guilty.

'It does matter,' he said as she bit into a piece of let-
tuce. 'Because that loss—my red card—set the Shadows
back years. In the past seven years they haven't made it
to another championship. They lost their chance at playing in an international league because of me. If I buy the
club I can change that. I *will* change that.'

'Yes, you will,' she said, seeing the determination in
his eyes.

But it made her worry about what her part in his plan
would cost her.

'Knowing what you know about my past...' She
cleared her throat. Reached for her wine when the action didn't do anything to help the sudden dryness that

was there. 'About my…insecurities, would you have still called me on to live TV today?'

A mixture of emotions played over his face. 'I… I don't know.'

There was a long pause.

'Why not?'

'Because there's a part of me that wants to protect you. But there's another part…'

'That wants this so badly you can't afford to protect me.'

It wasn't a question, but disappointment still soaked through her heart when there was another pause.

'I've wanted to prove myself for as long as I can remember. I've been working *seven years* for it.' He took a breath. 'I'll do everything I can to make sure you don't get hurt during this, Lily.'

She nodded, but couldn't reply.

'Lily, please.' Regret filled his voice. 'I'm sorry.'

'Don't apologise,' she answered, once the ache in her chest had subsided. 'You've been honest about your intentions. At least you have been this evening.' She exhaled shakily. 'I know this is important to you. And since you've been working so many years for it, it seems selfish to expect you to sacrifice it when you've only known me two days.'

'That's not…' He sighed. 'I don't know what to tell you, Lily. Except that it feels a hell of a lot longer than two days.'

He was struggling, she realised. It sent a shiver of hope through her. But then her mind offered her a look into the future.

She'd continue the charade with Jacques, convincing herself that he had feelings for her—developing feelings for *him*—deeper and more intense than anything she'd felt for Kyle. And then Jacques would get his club and he'd no longer need her.

And she would have to nurse the pain of the worst heartbreak of her life.

No, she thought, her heart aching even at the prospect of it. It was better to stop that hope from developing into something more dangerous now.

'Don't worry about me,' she said into the silence. 'I can look after myself.'

She could—and she would.

'You...you still want to do this? Even though—?'

'Yes,' she interrupted him. 'I'll still help you, Jacques.'

'Why?'

'Because it's time I faced my fears. And...because you need me to.'

She said nothing about reminding herself that there could be no hope for them.

'Have I told you how amazing you are?'

It was a line, she knew, but when she looked into his eyes she could almost believe it was true.

'Now, *darling*, there's no need for flattery. We're already dating, aren't we?'

CHAPTER FOURTEEN

AND SO THEY WERE.

For a month Lily dated Jacques Brookes. She went to charity events. Corporate events. She was wined and dined in Cape Town's most expensive restaurants. Showered with public displays of affection. Treated like royalty.

It was so similar to what she'd experienced with Kyle that she knew she should have pulled back. And if she'd *felt* anything similar to what she had when she'd been with Kyle maybe she would have.

But she didn't. Because there was one significant difference: Jacques.

The conversation they'd had the night they'd had dinner at the beach had clarified things. Lily knew what Jacques expected of her—knew why—and that made it easier to focus on their professional agreement. To lock away all those strange feelings that had been stirred the first two days they'd known each other.

She also couldn't deny that the attention their relationship got contributed to her focus. The pictures of them kissing on Jacques's balcony had been in the papers the day after they'd been taken. The photo of their 'intimate' dinner had been shared more than a hundred thousand times on social media after the waiter had posted it. Their interview snippet now had over a million views.

Their relationship had been sealed in public.

She didn't have time to think about personal feelings when she was dealing with all the interest in her. Customers now wanted pictures, signatures—though heaven only knew why they wanted them from *her*. She was just the girlfriend, not the actual celebrity.

When it became too much she reminded herself that she was facing her fears. She reminded herself that growth was never without pain. And she repeated that to herself when people began to poke into her past. When people who had never been her friends came forward to testify about how wonderful she'd been to them.

And, worst of all, when they discovered that she'd once been engaged to another of Cape Town's most eligible bachelors. The media had hounded her on that one, and more than one outlet had questioned the sincerity of her interest in Jacques.

Since that wasn't the kind of attention Jacques was hoping for, she'd expected him to step back. To tell her that he couldn't afford to be with someone who gave him negative press.

But he hadn't.

Instead he'd had his PR firm release a statement defending their relationship. He shut down any questions about her past when they were together, and held her tightly against him as he did so. As if he knew that she needed the comfort, the reassurance. And each time he would check that she was okay, Lily found that she was. Because although she would be shaking, Jacques would be holding her hand. Protecting her.

He'd said he would, and he'd kept his word.

And *that* was the real reason she was okay.

Jacques had even asked Jade from his PR firm to coach Lily when she could. So Lily knew what she shouldn't say in public—anything about Kyle except that they'd once been engaged and it hadn't worked out—and she knew what she should post on social media.

Those posts were strictly about Lily's, though, since Jade handled anything regarding Jacques and Lily's personal lives and their relationship. Still, Lily had seen an influx of 'likes' and 'follows' on the store's different accounts, and she knew that she would have to utilise them to keep momentum after her and Jacques's fake relationship ended.

That thought had caused a strange twinge in her heart lately, but she told herself it was because of the friendship she and Jacques had settled into. They'd got to know each other better over the dinners they'd shared, and Lily had got to see different sides of Jacques at different events. And sometimes after the events, Lily would watch his old games, his old interviews, and realise just how much he'd given up when his career had ended.

And then there were his business skills. Her respect for those grew whenever she saw him in action, and skyrocketed with everything he taught her about her own business. He'd taken her accounts, her business plan, and each time she saw him he gave her notes and guidelines. He pointed out where she had been going wrong—sometimes shockingly so.

It embarrassed her, and told her she shouldn't have opened a store before she had known all that, but never once did he make her feel like a failure. Even when her own thoughts mocked her—even when she would have fully understood if he called her that—he didn't. He just patiently told her where she should adjust, and how she should do so.

With those adjustments, and the increased traffic the store was getting, things were going surprisingly well. Despite the attention her relationship with Kyle had got, and despite those who called their relationship fake for the sake of Jacques's interest in the Shadows—those who saw through them—Lily was okay. Going out with Jacques was a little less intimidating every time she did it, and the clothes Jade would send her for events didn't scandalise her quite as much any more. Lily even found herself amused that for every one of those who doubted their relationship, ten others praised her for taming Bad-Boy Brookes.

So she ignored her worries. She ignored how, every time she spoke to her parents, she was reminded of the backlash she needed to anticipate when things with Jacques ended. How, every time she spoke to Caitlyn, she had to repeat that she didn't feel anything for Jacques other than friendship.

Because she didn't.

The niggle left behind after each of those conversations didn't mean anything.

And friends did sometimes pitch up at their friend's flats at five-thirty in the morning, Lily told herself as she did just that.

She hadn't been able to sleep the night before, and she suspected it was because she and Jacques would be attending one last event together that night, before Jacques made his bid for the club.

It had made her anxious—more than it should have—because she didn't want to lose her friend, she assured herself. So she'd got up at four, got ready for the day, and grabbed two coffees on her way to Jacques's flat. If she couldn't sleep, she could at least enjoy the sunrise.

With a friend. Who happened to have the perfect view to do that from...

She used the key he'd given her when he'd told her she could stay at his place on the nights she was working late. Between that and the events they were attending she was sometimes too exhausted to make the twenty-minute trip home. And, since Jacques's was less than half that time away, she'd found herself taking him up on his offer. But only the nights she knew he wouldn't be there. Lily wasn't sure she could handle staying in the same flat with him yet.

Yet?

She shook her head, forcing the thought away as she walked down the passage to Jacques's room. He was hosting the charity event that evening—for a Shadows-affiliated charity—at a venue in Big Bay, and had been staying at his Blouberg flat for the past week to see to the final arrangements.

When she got to his room, she pushed the door open softly.

And her heart just melted, pushing thoughts of friendship far away.

He lay on his back, one hand cushioning his head, the other on his bare chest. Though she appreciated the strength of his body—the defined chest, the chiselled abs, the full biceps—the unarmed expression on his face undid her. There was no guarded expression now, no worry lines, no indication that he was thinking about a million other things while he spoke to her.

Now he was just a man who slept. It made her realise, not for the first time, how much his plan required from him. And, while she understood the importance, she worried that it was going to break him in the process.

When she felt her chest tighten and her heart burn—

when she felt that neat little box she'd put her un-friend-like feelings about Jacques into tearing open—she took a shaky breath and walked towards him. She took no more than two steps before he shifted, turning his head in her direction. And though she stilled completely at the movement he opened his eyes, the sides of them crinkling with his smile when he saw her, as though her appearance was perfectly normal.

'Hi,' he said huskily, and her skin turned to goose-flesh.

'Hi,' she responded, and heard the hoarseness of her own voice—felt the intensity of her attraction for him edged with something more—and cleared her throat.

'I'm sorry I woke you, but I want to show you something.'

Now he frowned, and turned his head to the clock next to him.

'Lil, are you *kidding* me? It's not even six a.m. yet.'

Warmth spread through her body at his use of the nickname.

'No, I'm serious. Come to the living room.'

She turned to leave, eager to escape the tension that was rife in her body. It subsided—but only slightly—when she stood on his balcony, with the sight of the waves crashing on the shore and the salty air filling her lungs.

She handed him a coffee when she felt him next to her, saw that he had pulled on the shirt she assumed he'd worn the night before but hadn't closed it all the way, and cleared her throat again.

Forcing herself to focus on why she was there, she nodded her head in the direction of the sun. They didn't speak as they watched the sun slowly rise.

Lily wished she could spend more time appreciating the beauty of where she lived instead of worrying. Instead of feeling the constant fear of failure. She watched as the yellow and orange colours spread over the ocean, bringing light and warmth. And when the sun rose high enough that a ray lit over them she sighed, heard Jacques sigh, too.

She felt him move closer to her and she turned, tilting her head back to look up at him.

If she thought her heart had melted when she'd seen him asleep, she had no words to describe what was happening to it now.

'Is it wrong for me to want to kiss you?' he asked, taking the coffee from her hand and setting it on the table he'd added after her suggestion.

One of many things he'd done for her that made her heart melt a little more each time.

'Are there cameras around?' she replied softly, forcing herself to think of what was *real*.

'No.'

'Then why do you want to kiss me?'

He took her face in his hands gently, and it began to feel very real.

'Because you're beautiful. You're kind. You're just… you're amazing.'

She opened her mouth to deny it, but his lips were on hers before she could.

And then she was lost in the romance of kissing a man entirely too handsome to be interested in her.

On his balcony.

With the sun rising behind her.

And then she was lost in the kiss.

His lips felt as if they belonged on hers as they nudged. As they teased. As they sent warmth flowing through her body. And then his tongue joined hers, and she tasted the mint from his toothpaste, the coffee on his lips. She felt the temperature rise, the warmth now heat.

She put her hands on his waist, under the shirt he'd thrown on, and let them skim the sides of him. Her body responded when she felt his shudder, and she closed the distance between them so that she could memorise how those muscles would feel against her. So that when he realised he didn't really want her she would remember what it had been like to feel him against her.

To feel what it was like to have a man like Jacques want her.

He angled her so that she was pressed against the balcony railing, moaning when her hands slid over his abs and back down again. She couldn't think, couldn't breathe with his hands on her. She moved one of her own hands from where it explored his body, so that she could slide it through his hair as she'd wanted to do from the first night they'd met.

And then, when she felt him press even closer to her, she moved that hand to the base of his neck, wanting to taste more, to give more. A deep sound came from his throat, and pleasure thrilled her body at the thought that *she* was the one making him moan. That *she* was the one he was so greedily taking in.

He pulled back, and with fire in his eyes rasped, 'Stop me. Stop me now before we do something neither of us will be able to forget.'

'I don't want to stop,' she said, before reason could kick in.

Desire flared in his eyes as he dipped his head down towards her again.

His mouth was just a breath away when they heard a crash.

Jacques immediately shoved her behind him, but she

moved to see what the sound was, her heart beating hard for an entirely different reason now. At first she saw only a short man with dark hair, sprawled across a bin on the beach. The cause of their interruption. Then, when he pushed himself up, she saw the camera around the man's neck.

'He's taking pictures of us...' she breathed, and shock planted her feet to the ground before she willed herself to move.

She was in the house in the seconds it took for Jacques to take the steps down to the beach. A moment later she heard another crash that she wasn't entirely sure she wanted to know the cause of. She wrapped her jersey tightly around herself, stuffing her hands under her armpits to stop them shaking.

It was still strange to have someone take pictures of her. She was growing used to it at public events, but this kind—the kind that she couldn't prepare herself for, the kind that had photographers climbing fences to get their shot—still felt as if someone had told the world all her secrets.

And it succeeded in reminding her that real intimacy was out of the question for her and Jacques. She wasn't there to make memories she'd never forget. Memories that would probably haunt her for the rest of her life. She *had* to face reality, and that reality was that she was just a prop for Jacques. It made her wonder if he'd known about the camera. If he had kissed her *because* of it.

The hurt stunned her.

'Are you okay?' Jacques said when he walked into the house a few minutes later.

He slammed the doors shut, locked them, and pressed a button that tinted the clear glass.

'I'm... I'm fine.'

'Lily.' He took a step forward, and then stopped when she took one back. 'I took the memory card from his camera. He doesn't have any pictures of us.'

The words told her that he *hadn't* only been kissing her for the camera. And even if her mind still doubted it, her eyes saw that he held a small square memory card in his hand. She wanted to feel relief at that—should have—except that the fact that she'd doubted Jacques told her that she didn't quite trust him.

Was it because she knew those pictures would benefit him? Was that thought even fair? Jacques's actions over the past weeks had shown her that he was willing to protect her. That he was willing to risk losing publicity to do so. So why didn't she trust him?

Because the last man she'd trusted had hurt her, she thought.

And just as quickly she realised that she was scared the man she now loved would, too.

'I... I have to go. The shop...'

She couldn't say any more, too raw from the realisation.

'Okay...' Jacques replied slowly. 'Lil, can we just talk—?'

'No,' she said quickly.

The responding coolness in his eyes had her stuttering through an explanation.

'I'm... I'm already late. I have to go. I... I'm sorry.'

She didn't wait for him to speak. Instead she fiddled with the locks on the door and, when it opened, checked that there was no one else waiting to take her picture. When she was sure, she ran to her car.

She ran because more than anything else she wanted to stay.

And that terrified her.

CHAPTER FIFTEEN

I'll pick you up at seven.

THAT WAS IT. That was all Jacques's message had said. But it was seven now, and Lily had to stop herself from looking at the text message again to check whether she'd read it correctly. If she hadn't she would feel like an even bigger fool, standing there in her store—in front of its glass wall—in the scandalous dress Jade had sent her.

She and Jacques had decided—before the fiasco of that morning—to meet at her store, since the charity event's venue was around the corner from it. But as she looked down at the tight plunging neckline that pressed her breasts together, exposing more of them than the world had ever seen, she wondered if that had been a good idea. It seemed even worse when she considered the way the white dress hugged the curves of her body, barely brushing her knees and leaving nothing to the imagination.

Lily couldn't deny that the dress would draw attention to her and Jacques that night. And, while she had grown to be okay with Jade's other dress choices for that very reason, this one was the worst.

She smoothed at the non-existent creases, and then sighed. She was thinking about the dress because she didn't want to think about that morning. Just as she'd kept busy all day to avoid it. Lily was happy to brush her feelings under the carpet—maybe if she didn't pay attention to them they would go away.

Love doesn't just go away.

A rap on the door brought her from her thoughts—thankfully—and her throat dried when she saw Jacques. He was in a slim-cut navy blue suit, a white shirt open at the collar, his hair swept back in that untidy way she liked. His broad shoulders wore the stylish look effortlessly, his handsomely rugged features making him look so much more masculine—though she didn't know how that was possible.

Her body reminded her about the chance she'd missed with him, and she had to take a moment to compose herself before she opened the door for him.

'Hi,' she said, her knees going weak at the smell of his cologne.

'I'm sorry I'm late. Things were a bit busy today.'

His words were stilted. Clearly that morning wasn't going to be as easily forgotten as she'd hoped.

'That's fine.'

She turned away from him, letting him close the door behind him as she grabbed her handbag. When she looked at him again he was staring at her. Her face flushed.

'Jade was right.' His voice had softened. 'That dress does look amazing on you.'

'Thanks.'

She lifted a hand to her hair, and then brushed at her dress again.

'It's perfect,' he said. 'Lily, you're—'

He took a step forward and she moved back.

'Jacques, no.' She drew a breath. 'Please.'

'You're running.'

She lifted her eyes to his.

'From what? There's nothing to run from here,' she reminded him. *Herself.* 'We're just two people with an agreement, right?'

His eyes flashed. 'Where is this coming from? Things were fine—good, even—until—'

'Until this morning, when we kissed and almost did something to make things a little too real for the both of us?'

She could see that he hadn't expected her to verbalise it, but panic didn't give her a choice. And when he didn't answer her dread took its place, followed by something else that had her eyes burning.

'Let's just go,' she said, when she'd composed herself. 'It doesn't seem like we have anything to talk about anyway.'

She was pushing him away. And for the life of him he couldn't understand why.

Or why it bothered him so damn much.

Jacques grabbed two flutes of champagne from the nearest waiter as he walked into the venue where his charity event was being held. The room had a stunning three-hundred-and-sixty-degree view of the beach and the city through its glass walls—save for the end of the room that held the foyer. Still, it was a design unique to that hotel, which was precisely why he had chosen it.

He handed Lily a glass, and she smiled her thanks. But it wasn't her real smile. Over the past month he'd grown accustomed to the pretend smile she gave to photographers, to the public. He'd seen the smile she reserved only for people she cared about. The one where the skin around her eyes crinkled just a little. He'd seen it because in their private moments she'd aimed it at him.

The fact that she wasn't aiming it at him any more set him on edge. And that edge was quick to turn into anger. Because anger was easier than the longing he felt after their kiss that morning. Or the disappointment at her reaction to it.

Lily shifted next to him, reminding him of where he was, and he realised that she was uncomfortable. Public events weren't enjoyable for her, and unlike him, she wasn't accustomed to pretence.

The things he knew about her past made him realise there was more to it than that, of course, and though he'd already said it that night he repeated, 'You don't have to worry about how you look, Lily. You're gorgeous.'

She gave him an annoyed look.

'You *have* to say that, since your people sent me this ridiculous dress.'

His eyes moved over the white dress that clung to her body, desire trembling through his own.

'I approve of it.'

'Yes, you would. Your plan is more important than my insecurities, after all'

His focus on his plan had been dwindling because of her, so he said, 'That's not fair. You know it isn't.'

Vulnerability settled in her eyes. 'Maybe not. But it should be.'

'Jacques?'

He turned at the voice that interrupted his reply, and forced himself to greet Jade and Riley civilly.

'We're the first to get here,' he said, though it was through clenched teeth. 'I don't think I need to work the party just yet.'

'You *always* need to work the party,' Jade answered, and there was something in her voice that put his back up.

'What's going on?'

'I...er—' Jade glanced at Lily, and then back at Jacques. 'Actually, do you mind if I borrow Lily for a moment?'

His eyebrows rose, but he answered, 'Sure.'

Jade gave him a quick smile, and then hooked an arm in Lily's. Her height put her head barely at Lily's shoulders, making them a strange couple. He watched until they'd disappeared through the doors that led to the foyer and the bathrooms, and then turned back to Riley.

'What was that about?'

'She was trying to get Lily away from you,' Riley answered, and shifted his weight between his feet. 'We got news today that some of the sponsors still aren't convinced. About twenty per cent of them—the ones who aren't coming this evening—aren't prepared to stay on.'

'So?' he asked, refusing to let the panic settle in his chest. 'That's twenty per cent. We have the majority on our side.'

'They're the twenty per cent who contribute sixty per cent of the club's sponsorship.'

Riley named names, and Jacques swore under his breath. He knew exactly who they were—knew the club would take a huge knock if they pulled out.

'So what do we do?' he asked flatly.

'Well, we did some digging, and we think we can get some of them over to our side. They're family companies, and maybe if they see you as a family man...'

It took Jacques a moment to realise what Riley was saying.

'You want me to propose?'

Riley nodded. 'That was always our original suggestion. Of course we didn't anticipate all the good Lily would do to your reputation. People genuinely *like* her. Maybe if we had a bit more time...'

He trailed off, watched Jacques closely. And who could blame him? Jacques thought. He hadn't been open to that suggestion when they'd first made it. *And now you are?* an inner voice questioned, but he shook his head, refusing to dwell on it. Or on the panic about a possible marriage—even a fake one—that had his head spinning.

'How would I even *do* that? I mean, there's no time to arrange a proper proposal...'

Jacques stopped when Riley handed him a small blue box.

'You got a *ring*?' Jacques narrowed his eyes, his heart speeding up. 'How long have you two been planning this?'

'We only got the news today. But we thought tonight would be the perfect opportunity.'

The box felt heavier than anything he'd ever carried, and the weight of it sat on his chest. He stuffed it into his pocket, but that did no good either. He could still feel it there, throbbing against his thigh.

He had to talk to Lily about it. He couldn't do this to her after everything they'd shared. She didn't deserve—

His thoughts halted when he saw Kyle walk into the room.

'What's *he* doing here?' Jacques growled, and Riley shifted next to him.

'I... I don't know.'

'You and Jade *arranged* this event, Riley. How the hell don't you know?'

Anger had him clenching his fists as his eyes flitted between the space where he'd last seen Lily and Kyle.

'He must have bought someone else's ticket. His name wasn't on the guest list.'

'You'd better hope that's true.' Jacques turned to Riley.

'Because if I find out this was a scheme to get more money for this event…'

'It isn't,' Riley said quickly. 'We wouldn't do that.'

'I know that if this event is a success it's more likely that the club will come to me,' he said in a low voice. 'And that your firm will get a bonus for helping me secure it…'

'I promise, Jacques. This wasn't us.'

Though his colour was pale, Riley's voice was firm. It told Jacques he was telling the truth.

'I need to find Lily. Excuse me.'

'There's one more thing, Jacques.'

He was already on his way to find Lily, but he turned back impatiently.

'What is it, Riley? I don't have the luxury of time, here.'

His eyes were searching the room for Kyle, but with Riley's single sentence everything in Jacques's body froze.

'Nathan called us a few hours ago to let us know he'll be bringing your father as his plus one.'

CHAPTER SIXTEEN

'WHAT ARE THE chances of us meeting like this?'

Lily thought she was imagining his voice at first. She'd escaped from where Jade had been introducing her to guests in the foyer to the bathrooms. But on her way there, she'd realised it wouldn't have given her the privacy she'd hoped for and had headed to the conference room instead.

But now she turned and saw Kyle, and realised two things. One, he must have followed her, and two, his voice hadn't been her imagination.

'I think the chances were always going to be pretty high, since you must have seen me come in here.'

'I see you've worked on that confidence problem since I last saw you.'

Warning coated his tone, but Lily braced herself against the inevitable fear. And, though it wasn't easy, she found she could do it.

'Why are you here?'

'To see you.' He took a step closer and her breath almost caught. 'To remind you of your place.'

'Don't you have someone else to remind now?'

The bravado was a farce, but it was her only defence.

'I don't have to remind Michelle of her place. She knows exactly what I need from her.'

'I still don't understand,' she said a little desperately. 'Why are you here?'

She wanted him to get to the point. Because the sooner he did, the sooner she would be able to escape.

'I've seen pictures of you and Jacques together,' Kyle spat. 'You're disgracing yourself. And making *me* look bad.'

'That's not true.'

'You were *my* fiancée, Lily. And everyone knows that now. So start acting like someone worthy of being associated with my name.'

'No one cares about me and you, Kyle,' she said, unable to help herself. 'All they're interested in is Jacques. If I need to act appropriately for the sake of anyone's name it would be Jacques's and not yours.'

There was a pulse of silence, and then Kyle closed the space between them. Instinct had her moving back, every brave part of her fading into the fear that had her heart in her throat. A part of her mind was telling her she could simply escape the event if Kyle bruised her, another was formulating the apology she would have to give to Jacques if someone saw her leave.

But she didn't have time to think about it any further. The door opened and in a few quick movements Jacques was in front of Kyle.

'You should leave. Before I remind you of what my fist feels like.'

Lily didn't think she'd ever heard anything sound as menacing. And, considering the look on Kyle's face, she didn't think he had either.

'She's after your money. Just like she was after mine.'

The air in her lungs quite simply froze. But Jacques didn't respond to Kyle's words. Instead he said, 'I'm going to say this one more time, and then I'm going to act on it. And, no, I *don't* care if people speculate about it when they see you leave with a bloody face.'

Jacques sent Kyle a hard look.

'They're all aware of my reputation.' There was a short pause, and then Jacques repeated, 'Leave—before I make you leave.'

Kyle didn't stay any longer to tempt fate, and when he was gone Lily's knees went weak. In one quick movement Jacques's arms were around her, steadying her.

'It's okay,' he said softly. 'He's gone. And he won't be back.'

'How do you know?'

'Because I told you I would protect you. And that means making sure Kyle never gets to you again.'

At his words, she rested her head on his chest and for a brief moment closed her eyes. She wished they could stay like that, away from the realities of the world. But she knew they couldn't. Not when Kyle's presence had reminded her of something she'd managed to avoid thinking about in the past month. Not when she knew Jacques would ask her about it.

She took a step back, asked a question to delay the inevitable. 'How did you know where we were?'

'I saw him arrive, and then I got distracted.' A shadow passed over his face. 'When I couldn't find him again—or you—I began to look for you. And then I found you.'

'Thank you.'

'What was he talking to you about?'

She turned her back towards him, needing the time to compose herself. She told herself she needed to do this—not because Jacques had asked, but because *she* needed to tell him.

She needed to do this for herself.

When she turned back, he was watching her with expressionless eyes.

'When I found Kyle cheating on me I was devastated. Not because I loved him—which I realised after a few weeks—but because it gave my insecurities more grounds than they'd had in a long time.'

Her voice faltered with those words, but she cleared her throat.

'And although Kyle begged me to go back to him—though he told me that he'd just made a mistake—I couldn't believe him. You don't make a mistake like that when you love someone.'

Get to the point, she told herself.

'When he realised I wasn't coming back he began to buy me things. And when I sent them back he told me I could have whatever I wanted. That it would be my "choice".'

Bitterness washed over her tongue.

'And when *that* didn't work he threatened me.'

She saw the fist Jacques made in response to her words, stifled the hope that flared inside her. It didn't mean anything.

'I told him if he didn't stop I would go to the police, and I was on the way there when his family's lawyer called me.' She took another breath—for courage. 'He wanted a meeting. He told me that the Van der Rosses wanted to "solve" the situation without involving the police, and that he would ensure Kyle stayed away from me. By then I just… I just wanted it all to go away.'

She still cursed her naiveté.

'So I agreed to the meeting, and when I got there Kyle's parents were there, too. They were never…fond of me. They thought I was beneath their son, that I was too dowdy, too…common.'

And she'd proved them right, she thought with a pang.

'Though they were perfectly nice to me. Told me they were so sorry about how everything had ended with me and Kyle.'

The rest came out as a rush. She couldn't bear the silence, the tension that pulsed from Jacques.

'And then they told me that they'd give me whatever I wanted if I signed a non-disclosure agreement. I just had to agree never to speak about Kyle's philandering ways—especially since his father was pitching to an important client with solid family values—and I could ask them for anything.'

'And so you asked for money?'

The flat tone broke her heart.

'I didn't. Not at first. I asked them why they thought it was necessary. Whether they really thought I would ruin their business because Kyle had broken my heart. And my self-confidence, which was really the case.'

She closed her eyes, and then shrugged.

'Though they only actually said something about "covering all their bases", I realised that it was because they didn't think much of me. The look on his mother's face... I knew what they thought of me, and it made me feel so...*worthless*.'

She bit her lip, tried to stop the tears from coming.

'So I asked for something that would make that feeling go away.'

She paused now, and looked at Jacques's face. His expression made her attempts not to cry useless, and she brushed at the tears.

'My store,' she continued when she'd cleared her throat, 'was something I'd been working on for years. I knew I would never have enough money to start it if I didn't take the money from them. So we agreed on an amount and I signed the document.'

So now he knew, she thought, and folded her arms as she waited for him to respond.

'That's why you didn't want to take the loan I offered you?'

'Yes.'

There was a pause.

'I have to propose to you.'

'What?'

He shoved his hands into his trouser pockets. 'I don't have the Shadows' most important sponsors on my side. Riley told me that they might be swayed if I propose to you.'

'And you...what? Want my permission?'

'Yes.' His tone was clipped. 'I didn't want to put you on the spot again.'

Her heart wanted to soften at his words. At the confirmation that things between them had changed. That *he'd* changed. But how could it when he couldn't even look her in the eye?

'I appreciate you asking me. And...and I know this is important to you. So of course I agree.'

'Thank you.'

He nodded and then turned away.

'Jacques, please. Say something. Anything. Tell me you're disappointed in me. That you can't stand it that I took money from them.'

He turned back. 'Is that how you feel about yourself?'

A sob escaped from her lips. *'Yes.'*

'Would you do it again?'

'I didn't even want to take a loan from *you*, Jacques. You know the answer to that.'

'Why not?'

'Because taking that money has stripped away my confidence, my self-worth.' She was purging herself now, she thought. 'Because I've belittled my success by taking it. Because the lack of success in the months before I met you eroded every belief I'd had that owning my shop would make me feel better. That it would make me feel like I was more than what other people thought me.'

It would have felt *so* good if she'd finally been able to make a success of something. If she'd finally been able to prove her parents wrong. The engagement had been the only thing they'd approved of in her life, and she'd disappointed them once again when she'd told them it had ended.

She hadn't told them Kyle had cheated on her. It wouldn't change the fact that they saw her as a failure. That she saw *herself* that way...

'Oh, here you are.'

Jade popped her head into the room, and her smile faltered as she looked from Lily to Jacques.

'I'm sorry, I've interrupted something...'

'What do you want, Jade?' Jacques asked tersely.

'I was actually checking to see if this room was free, not looking for you. Yet. But there *are* a few people...' She trailed off. 'I can stall them if you like?'

'No, that's fine,' Lily said. 'I'll go.'

She avoided Jacques's gaze as she walked out of the room, too embarrassed by her confession to look at him.

She spent a few minutes in the bathroom, composing herself and freshening up.

When she returned to the event she thought she could fake her way through trivial conversation. Until her eyes settled on Nathan and something inside her sagged with relief.

'It's nice to see a familiar face here.' She kissed him on the cheek.

'I know how you feel,' Nathan answered, but when he gave her a smile it seemed distracted. 'It's almost like old times.'

His eyes shifted over the room and she remembered that Caitlyn wasn't with him. That she wouldn't be for the rest of the night.

'I didn't think you would come without Cait. She told me she had a deadline for tomorrow morning.'

'I wasn't going to. But I changed my mind last minute.'

'Did you bring Kyle?'

'What?' Nathan's attention was now on her. 'Kyle's *here*?'

'He was.'

'Are you okay?'

'Yes,' she answered, and found that it was true. 'Your brother helped.'

And that was the reason she was okay.

'Is Kyle still alive?'

She smiled, though she could tell Nathan was only half-joking.

'He is. But he won't be bothering me again.' She was pretty sure of that.

There was a moment of silence and then Nathan closed his eyes. 'Lily, I didn't bring him, but I think he was here tonight because of me. I mentioned it to him earlier today. I'd just decided to come, and was telling him I couldn't work late on a case. I'm so sorry!'

'It's okay.' Her heart was beating at its normal rate again. 'It worked out in the end.'

And she needed to find the man who'd ensured that. They needed to talk.

'Will you excuse me, Nate? I have to find…'

Her voice stopped working when she saw a man walking towards them. Dark skin, dark hair peppered with white, a strong, muscular build. If it hadn't been for the fact that he was clearly years older Lily might have thought she was looking at Jacques. And then, when he stopped in front of them, she saw Nathan's face.

Her heart began to thrum uncomfortably in her chest.

'Dad,' Nathan said, confirming her suspicions. 'This is Lily. Caitlyn's best friend and—'

'Jacques's girlfriend.'

His deep voice held a hint of an accent—British, she thought—and it reminded her, again, of Jacques. But there was something beneath the tone that sounded off to her.

You're bringing your feelings for Jacques into this, an inner voice told her, but she shook it off. It was too complicated a thought to consider before introducing herself.

She smiled and offered a hand. 'Yes. It's lovely to meet you, Mr Brookes.'

'Please, call me Dale,' he said, and brought Lily's hand to his mouth.

A shimmer of discomfort went down her spine, but again she shook it off.

'Does Jacques know you two are here?' she asked pleasantly, directing her question at Nathan.

She saw something that might have been shame pass through his eyes—he clearly knew she was actually referring to whether Jacques knew his *father* was there—before he shook his head.

'I don't think so, no. I haven't seen him yet.'

Suddenly it made sense to Lily. Nathan had been looking for Jacques. To warn him? No, she thought. He could have called him to do that. This was some kind of...*ambush*, she thought, and anger simmered through her veins.

'I should probably find him, then,' she said, and heard the coldness in her stilted tones.

'Are you looking for me, my love?'

An arm snaked around her waist, pulling her closer until she was moulded to Jacques's body.

'Yes, I was.'

She brushed a piece of hair away from his face and he looked down at her, just as she'd intended. He smiled, but by now she knew when it wasn't genuine. Even if she hadn't been able to tell she would have known it by the hard glint in his eyes.

'Well, I'm here now.' He turned his head to the two men in front of him. 'And I see Nathan's introduced you to my father.'

There was a pause.

'Why are you here, *Dad*?' He said the word in a mocking tone.

'I heard you needed some help with your…*investment.*'

Dale had used the same tone as Jacques, and Lily felt Jacques's arm tighten around her.

'You told him that?' Jacques asked Nathan after a moment.

Lily saw Nathan's slight nod, saw the apologetic look in his eyes. It told her that maybe Nathan hadn't meant to ambush Jacques. Maybe he'd wanted a reconciliation. But that didn't seem to be the direction their conversation was going in.

'Well, I don't need your help. Haven't needed it in a very long time, if I recall.'

'Yes, the success of your rugby career tells me how *well* you're doing in your life.'

The muscles under Lily's hand hardened, coiled, as if she was touching an animal that was about to pounce.

'My rugby career may not have ended in the way I

had hoped for, but it made me into a much better man,' Jacques replied in a measured tone. 'I'm going to buy my club—without your help—and I'm going to turn it into something I never could have while I was just playing for it.'

Determination fortified every word, sending pride bursting through her body.

'Trying to convince me, son, or yourself?'

'That's the trouble with you, Dad. You never really got to know me,' Jacques said easily. 'If you had, you'd know I never say things unless I believe them. It's called *conviction*—though you wouldn't really be familiar with the word.'

His arm dropped from Lily's waist, and he took her hand instead.

'You'd also know that I no longer feel the need to convince you of anything.'

With those words, Jacques pulled at her hand and they walked away.

CHAPTER SEVENTEEN

THERE WAS NO time for him to process his thoughts. There hadn't been since Jade had interrupted his conversation with Lily. And now he had his feelings about Lily's revelation and seeing his father again swirling through his head—all before he needed to speak to the people who held his fate in their hands.

'Stop.'

Lily tugged at his hand, stopping him in a relatively empty corner of the room.

'I have my speech soon. And the proposal...'

She drew in a breath at his words, but shook her head and then angled him so that his back was to the crowd.

'I know. But you have to take a moment to breathe. Pretend you're stealing an intimate moment with the woman who's about to be your fiancée.'

She was right—he needed to breathe. He needed to deal with the rush of emotions that was making him feel nauseous *before* he spoke to the crowd.

Suddenly he became aware of the way his chest was heaving, and because he didn't want to be he focused on Lily. 'I heard the way you said "fiancée". It scares you.'

'Of course,' she answered breathily. 'Doesn't it scare you?'

'No.' *Yes.* 'It's not real.'

'Someone should tell my heart that,' she murmured. Her eyes widened and she quickly followed that with, 'It's beating so fast at the prospect.'

Focusing on her words—on the possibility of what they might mean—was helping to distract him. 'Mine is, too.'

'You don't have to say that to make me feel better.'

'I'm not.' And he realised he wasn't.

'I thought you weren't scared?'

'I'm not. But that doesn't mean I'm not nervous.'

As he said it he realised that there was more to his confession. That it coated something he didn't fully understand yet.

'I'm sorry for the way things turned out tonight,' she said.

'It's okay,' he answered, and looked down at her.

As he did so, he realised that he'd been avoiding it since she'd told him about accepting money from Kyle's family. His heart immediately softened—he worried that it had weakened—and he felt the disappointment that he'd felt at her words disappear.

That was why he'd avoided looking at her. Because though her confession should have made him doubt her—he had experience with people who thought money was the most important thing, after all—he didn't. He *couldn't.*

And he found himself feeling even more for her.

'Is it really okay?' She shook her head. 'Kyle pitches up here, and then your father. It's like the past is trying to make sure we remember it.'

She gave him a small smile.

'For what it's worth, I'm really proud of you. I was worried at first. I saw your face when you joined us. But then you *spoke* and I could tell it was just occurring to you. I was so proud.'

He felt as if her words had switched on a light in his body. It warmed him even as it pulsed in his chest, and he realised that the desire to hear those words from his father had driven him through most of his life. Even when he'd been convincing his mother to leave he'd still wanted to hear it.

And though he'd realised long ago that it wasn't going to happen he hadn't accepted it. Not until he'd heard Lily say it and felt that desire go free inside him.

'It looks like you're up,' Lily said, nodding her head to where Jade was trying to get Jacques's attention.

He gave Jade a quick nod, and then tried to formulate something to say to Lily. But he found he couldn't. His brain was a mess from the things he felt, and from those he thought he should feel but didn't.

So he focused on his responsibilities. They'd become too vague for his liking, and the urgency of the plan he had been so set on had faded into the background over the past month. But tonight would change that, he told himself a little desperately. He would put all the distractions aside and charm whoever he needed to.

Starting with that proposal.

'Thank you, Tom,' Jacques said, when the MC handed him the mike after his introduction. 'Let's all give Tom a hand. He's doing a terrific job, hosting this evening's proceedings.'

Applause rang out and Jacques's eyes moved over the crowd. His gaze settled on Nathan, who was standing alone on one side of the room, shoulders hunched. Though Jacques was still angry with him, he knew his brother had just wanted to help.

But, considering that Jacques no longer saw his father, he also knew that Nathan's attempt at reconciliation hadn't worked. Just as Jacques had always told him.

He went through the formalities, thanking everyone for attending and introducing the charity they were supporting that evening. While a representative for the charity said her thanks, Jacques's heart started beating faster. As he handed the woman a large cheque and posed for the required photos his lungs felt heavy. And when he finally held the mike in his hand to end his speech his entire body shook.

But he ignored all of it, and focused on the face of the woman he was about to fake propose to.

'I know many of you here remember me as the man who ended the Shadows' path to the internationals. The man who threw away his career in a fight that shouldn't have happened. It's shaped your opinion of me. And *that* has shaped my opinion of myself.'

His heart thudded for different reasons now.

'It has also driven me. Because I wanted to prove...'

He trailed off, thinking about how he'd wanted to prove that the public's opinion of him was wrong. How he'd wanted to prove his father wrong.

'I wanted to prove that I was more than the mistakes I'd made. That those mistakes didn't define me. That desire has allowed me to build a successful company. It's given me a perspective that's helped me support charities like the one we're here for this evening. But, most importantly, my journey in not letting the past define me has led me to my girlfriend, Lily.'

The first thing he saw when his eyes rested on her was that colour on her cheeks that had drawn him in the first time. The second was the smile she sent him. Though the uncertainty, the traces of fear, were visible to him, it was the sweetest, most encouraging smile he'd ever seen.

And the words that came from his mouth no longer seemed to be pretence.

'There have been times when I've focused so much on *wanting* to be a better person that I haven't actually *been* a better person. And she has helped me see that. Her calling me out on my bad behaviour has given me no choice but to learn from the past. Which is probably why you have all seen a better-behaving Brookes instead of Bad-Boy Brookes.'

He waited as a chuckle went through the crowd.

'But perhaps more importantly is the fact that she's *shown* me how to learn from my past.'

He thought about how she'd refused his money—taking it would certainly have been easier than the training she'd asked for instead—and about how it made sense now that he knew about Kyle.

'I wish you could see yourself the way I see you.'

He walked down the stairs towards Lily now, taking the microphone with him.

'You would be able to see your strength, your beauty.'

A path opened up as he walked towards her, and when he stopped in front of her he could see the hope shining through her uncertainty. It scared him, and something urged him to stop. But he couldn't. Not yet.

'And you'd know that you've exceeded any expectations I had of you or our relationship.'

He knew how much those words would mean to her, but when her hope shone even brighter it glossed all his feelings with a deep fear he couldn't understand.

'I can't imagine my life without you, Lily,' he said, almost automatically now, refusing to hear the truth of the words.

Instead he pulled out the box Riley had given him earlier and went down on one knee.

'Will you marry me?'

CHAPTER EIGHTEEN

I T WASN'T UNTIL that moment that Lily realised just how much she wanted him to be saying those words for real.

The desire for it shook her, but she didn't let it distract her. She breathed a 'yes' and applause erupted around them. Jacques smiled at her, but there was a storm in his eyes that made her heart hurt without her even knowing why.

He slid the ring onto her finger—a simple stunning solitaire—and pulled her into his arms. Heat pricked at her eyes when she felt the stiffness of his arms, the tightness of the muscles in them, but all the years she'd had of pretending to be okay when she wasn't helped her smile and accept the kiss he brushed on her lips.

The rest of the evening went by in a blur of congratulations and a tension that she knew she wasn't imagining. Not when she could sense Jacques pulling away from her. Not when she recognised it because she'd done the exact same thing herself earlier. And while a part of her wanted to hope that they were doing it for the same reason—that he was in love with her, too—Jacques's behaviour was edged with a coldness that warned her against hoping that.

The thought troubled her so much that she escaped the party as soon as she saw an opportunity to do so. Her opportunity came when Jade and Riley whisked Jacques away to speak to a sponsor they apparently needed on their side who'd arrived unexpectedly. The crowd had thinned by then, and no one seemed to notice as she slipped out of the hotel to the beach just beyond it.

When she was far enough away that no one would see her—when she was sure that she hadn't been followed— she closed her eyes and accepted the truth that she'd been running away from since that morning.

She was in love with Jacques Brookes.

Panic gripped her throat, and when she opened her mouth to breathe a sob escaped. She laid a hand on her throat, forced air into her lungs. Forced herself to think. Why was she afraid of falling for Jacques? Because she'd told herself that she needed to stay away from him? That she needed to love herself?

Perhaps, but she knew those resolutions had come from the Lily who'd been treated so poorly by her ex-fiancé. By the Lily who'd thought she deserved to be treated that way. Who had *expected* it because she didn't think she deserved more. But that Lily had slowly been whittled away. She'd been replaced with a Lily who hoped that she *did* deserve more. She'd been replaced with a Lily who had experienced what it was like to be treated well. Who had experienced a good relationship for the past month.

Yes, it had been a pretend relationship for the most part, but Lily thought that their *friendship* hadn't been pretend. The respect they'd shared, the way Jacques had treated her, the things he'd said to her, about her—those hadn't been pretend.

Or had they?

Didn't Jacques deserve more than her? Didn't he deserve someone who was proud of her body, of herself?

Someone with all the confidence that *she* struggled to muster? Someone who felt as if she were enough? Someone who could actually live up to his expectations?

Someone who could live up to her *own* expectations?

She was reminded of when Jacques had asked her about those expectations. She'd realised she didn't *have* expectations of herself—not her own. She only had those that had been invented by those around her.

But now she knew she wanted to be successful. For herself and not just to prove someone else wrong. She wanted to think more of herself. It would be a process, but at least now she believed that she deserved more than an emotionally abusive fiancé. She wanted someone who saw her as more than who *he* wanted her to be. She wanted someone who saw her for who she was.

She wanted Jacques.

And if she ignored her uncertainties—if she looked at the facts, at the evidence—she thought that he wanted her, too.

But he didn't want to.

'Lily? I've been looking all over for you.'

She turned to the man she loved. Saw the look on his face, saw the confirmation of her suspicions, and her heart broke.

'I'm sorry. I needed some air.'

The words sounded distant—as if she was pulling away again—and the door he'd hidden his feelings behind opened.

He slammed it shut.

'Did things go well with the sponsor?'

'I think so. They asked about my plans for the club.'

'Which is a *good* thing, right? It means they're considering your business aptitude and not your personal life.'

'Yeah, probably. But Jade and Riley think my personal life is the reason they were interested. They think the sponsors caught the proposal.'

'That was the plan, wasn't it?'

'Yes, it was.'

So why was he annoyed by her response? By her sudden aloofness?

'It's all there is, isn't it?' Jacques said through a clenched jaw. 'This plan of ours. This *agreement*.'

She tilted her head, and it stole his breath how much he wanted to tuck those curls behind her ear. How he wanted to pull her in and melt that coolness.

'Are you trying to bait me, Jacques?'

'What could I possibly achieve by doing that?'

'My temper? I could lash out at you and give you a reason to deny those feelings you've realised you had for me.'

'I don't... There are no...'

'No feelings?'

'No.'

She laughed. 'Of course. There were no feelings when we kissed this morning. Or when you said those things tonight. No, that kiss actually *was* for the camera. And tonight—that was just for the audience, right?'

'Now you're trying to bait *me*.'

'Is it working? Because I'd really *love* to talk to the man I've fallen in love with instead of whoever *you* are.'

It took him a minute to process what she'd said. Another to think up a response. 'How...? You can't...'

'I don't blame you for thinking that.' She folded her arms, looked out to the ocean. 'I've been trying to deny it since this morning, when I realised it.'

'Since this morning?' he repeated.

Now he knew why he'd felt her pulling away. She didn't like her feelings any more than he liked his.

Why did that upset him?

'We always knew about the attraction between us,' he said steadily.

'The *attraction*?' she scoffed. 'I *wish* this was just an attraction. That would make things *so* much easier.'

'What do you want from me, Lily?'

'I want you to admit that there's more between us than an "attraction". I want you to admit you feel something for me.'

That door he kept those feelings behind vibrated again, and he was having trouble keeping it shut.

'You don't want that, Lily. You're just confusing all of the...the show with real emotion.'

You're making up excuses for yourself.

'Don't do that.'

Her voice was measured, but he could hear the anger.

'Don't belittle my feelings. I've spent my life trying to convince myself that I have a right to them.'

'I wasn't trying—'

'Do you think I *wanted* to tell you the truth about my store? About Kyle? Do you think that I told you how it made me feel because we're *friends*? Because we're attracted to each other?' She shook her head. 'No one knew about that. And not just because of the papers I signed.'

'Then why did you tell me?'

'Because I thought you would understand. You know what it's like to think about your past with shame. This whole charade has been so that you could make up for it. I wanted your help with my store for the same reason.'

She drew a ragged breath.

'And I told you because I wanted you to know. To love me despite my mistakes.'

The door was flung open at her words, and he knew that he *did* love her. He knew that he'd known from the moment they'd kissed. That he'd had it confirmed while he'd been proposing.

But still he couldn't bring himself to say the words.

Instead he said, 'I meant it when I said you've shown me how to not let the past define me.' He exhaled. 'I don't judge you for accepting the money. I can't because…because I *do* understand it. The shame. The determination not to let a mistake define you.'

'But?'

'But…you've distracted me from it.'

'I've distracted you from what?'

'From my *plan*,' he said desperately. 'From showing the world that I'm more than my mistakes. Than my failures. Than the disappointment.'

'Showing the world or your father?'

He didn't respond. He couldn't. Because she was right.

'Seeing him tonight reminded you that you've been doing all of this for *him*, not the world. That all those things—mistakes, failures, disappointment—are things you're trying to convince *him* that you're not. And maybe even yourself.'

'Stop!' he said sharply, feeling her words piercing his heart.

'I understand it, Jacques.' She moved closer to him. 'I'm trying to convince myself that I'm not those things either. That *I'm* not a failure.'

'You're only a failure because *you* keep telling yourself that, Lily.'

The words were harsher than he'd intended, but he just wanted her to stop. To stop reminding him of the pain he'd managed to avoid for so long. He didn't listen to the voice telling him that it wasn't Lily, that it was seeing his father that had unlocked the pain. All he knew was that he *felt*—and *she* was making him feel.

He couldn't distinguish between the feelings. Not any more.

'You keep thinking about the things you've failed at. But have you looked at what you've *succeeded* at? You had problems with your weight, so you lost it. You had a relationship that you realised wasn't working for you, so you left. The shop you opened was struggling, so you found a way to make it work for you. Yes, you've failed. You've made mistakes. We *all* have. But we need to look at how we've dealt with the failure and mistakes. *That's* what defines us.'

There was silence after his little speech, and he realised his chest was heaving. He used the time to gain control of his breathing again—to gain control of *himself* again.

'Are you going to look back at this night and think it's a mistake, Jacques?' Her voice was soft. Deceptive. 'Because if you can't give me a reason to stay, to listen to the things you're saying, you might find something else to define yourself by.'

CHAPTER NINETEEN

LILY DIDN'T KNOW what she expected after her words. All she knew was that she didn't have to stay—not any more—if there was nothing to stay for.

But she knew she hadn't expected a kiss.

He was standing in front of her before she could register what was happening, and then he slid a hand behind her neck and pulled her in until his mouth found hers. Heat immediately flared at the touch, but the greed their kisses had held before had been replaced by emotion. She didn't know what it meant—didn't know if he was telling her he had feelings for her or if he was saying goodbye.

She pulled back. She didn't need any more memories of him if it was goodbye.

'I need you to *say* it, Jacques.'

'I… I can't.'

He rested his forehead on hers, but she stepped back, unable to stand being near him any more.

'Why not?'

She hated the heat that prickled in her eyes. Hated it even more that her heart softened as she saw the battle on his face. But she *had* learnt from her mistakes. And that meant she could no longer hope for things in a relationship that she would never get. She could no longer stay with someone who couldn't be honest with her. She deserved more.

So when he didn't answer she didn't make any excuses. She just cleared her throat and said, 'We'll have Jade leak a story that we've gone away to celebrate our engagement. Just for the two days before you make your bid for the club. I'll let Terri and Cara know, and they can take care of the store for me. And then you can make your bid, get your club, and people will see us less and less. An appropriate amount of time will go by and we'll announce our break-up.'

'Lily, please—'

'No, Jacques. I know better than anyone what you're willing to do when you really want something. And if that something was me, you'd be able to say so.'

It hurt, the truth of that realisation. But she needed to face it.

'It's the least I deserve after doing all this for you.'

Because she had to believe that, she walked away from him. She only stopped to slip her shoes back on in front of the hotel, and then climbed into the first taxi she saw. She kept her composure until she reached her flat. Until she stripped off that ridiculous dress, kicked off those ridiculous shoes and climbed into the shower.

And then she let the tears come.

They turned into heart-wrenching sobs too quickly, but they helped steady her. And when the water turned cold she *felt* steadier. She let the water wash the tears from her face and then focused on the rest of her body. When she was done, she made herself a cup of tea, gripping the mug for the warmth and comfort it provided.

She was proud of herself. There was an ache in her chest that grew more painful with each beat of her heart, but she was proud. From the moment she'd met Jacques she'd told herself she couldn't be interested in him—in anyone, really—until she knew her self-worth.

It was the only way she knew how to survive what she'd been through with Kyle.

How to ensure that it would never happen again.

She couldn't be treated the way Kyle had treated her again. She couldn't be manipulated as she'd been by his parents. She wanted to think of herself without shame, without disgust. And the only way she knew how to do that was to stand up for herself.

Jacques hadn't treated her the way Kyle had. And after that night at the beach he'd no longer manipulated her. But in her heart she knew that if she'd accepted the little that Jacques had offered her she would have been undermining her worth again. She wouldn't have been standing up for herself, or for the love she now believed she deserved.

So she was proud of herself.

Even when a voice taunted her that she'd failed at *this* too she stayed proud. And she banished those thoughts by remembering the way Jacques's face had glowed with something he didn't even know when he'd proposed.

It had made her almost believe he'd meant all those things he'd said to her. That she *had* been showing him how to learn from the past. That maybe her determination to do that *had* been an example to him. Even if she hadn't always succeeded, she'd tried. And wasn't that something?

And maybe she could believe that he thought she was strong—something she'd never thought of herself before. And that she was beautiful—something she'd never given herself a chance to believe before. But what had meant the most was what he'd said about her exceeding his expectations—something she'd never, ever experienced before.

She hadn't even cared that everybody had been looking at her. The only thing she'd seen was that look on Jacques's face...

She stilled.

She hadn't cared that everybody had been looking at her.

That was in such stark contrast to what she'd felt only a month ago at the television show. Then, she'd *hated* the thought of people looking at her in normal clothing. But tonight she hadn't cared that everybody had been looking at her in a tight dress. She hadn't been thinking about what anyone might have thought about how she looked in it. She hadn't cared about her weight.

It was a victory she'd never thought possible. A victory that she knew had come from the time she'd spent with Jacques. His easy acceptance of her, his compliments, the way he'd forced her to see herself as he did—even if it had been harsher than she would have liked, she thought as she remembered what he'd told her that night—it had all been part of the reason she was in love with him.

It was the reason she'd laid everything on the line and told him how she felt.

Though she'd thought them all gone, another tear fell down her cheek.

Had she given up the man who'd shown her how to love herself?

Were the reasons she had worth the sacrifice?

She didn't know. But when things had ended with Kyle she'd promised herself she would learn from the experience. And she knew she had. But, as Jacques had told her, she needed to stop dwelling on the past. She needed to learn from it and move on.

She could no longer expect to fail. She could no longer accept others' expectations of herself as her own. She needed to stand firm in her confidence, in her newly dis-covered self-worth. She needed to stop letting her past mistakes define her.

She would pay back the money, she told herself. It didn't matter that it might take years. What mattered was that paying it back would allow her to take back the integrity she'd lost. What mattered was that she would finally be able to appreciate her hard work, her success, if she did.

What will you learn after Jacques? an inner voice asked.

Lily closed her eyes. What she'd learnt *during* her time with Jacques was easy, she thought.

But all she had for after was a pain in her chest, mock-ing her for thinking she could move on to 'after' at all.

Jacques wondered if he would ever forget how it had felt when Lily had walked away from him on the beach. How it had felt to know he had feelings for her but being un-able to say it.

It had been two days and he hadn't forgotten it.

Hell, not even the news that he'd got the club had ban-ished the memory.

He'd given it time. He'd thought that maybe the mis-ery of the past two days had just delayed the excitement, the happiness. But it had been nearly five hours now, and the satisfaction of getting everything he'd always wanted was still missing.

Because it was only what you thought you wanted.

He pushed up from the table he'd put on his balcony after Lily had suggested it to him. It was true. He'd *be-lieved* he'd wanted the club. He'd believed it so much that he'd resisted his feelings for Lily because she'd dis-tracted him from it. Because she'd distracted him from the plan that had driven him for *seven years*: to ensure that he wasn't defined by his failures, by his mistakes.

Or by the man who loved money more than his own children.

Jacques's fingers tightened on the balcony railing he was leaning against.

He'd spent so much of the past seven years trying to prove his father wrong. But the truth was that Jacques had also been trying to prove that who his father was didn't define *him*. That the man who would tell his son he could never mean as much to his mother as *he* did—who would call his son a failure and a disappointment—didn't dictate who Jacques would become.

When he'd realised he had treated Lily in those first two days when they'd met like his father had treated his mother, something had shifted inside Jacques. And he'd seen a change in himself over the past month. He hadn't cared as much about his plan as he had about Lily. His wish for the world to see him as someone better than he'd once been had become less important than him being better for Lily.

And then he'd seen his father, and he'd been able to stand up to him. He'd been able to set aside his feelings for the parent who'd dismissed him—who'd been the reason his mother had dismissed him, too—and he'd bought his club, just as he'd told his father he would.

He'd thought it had been possible because he'd changed so much over the seven years since he'd last seen the man. But the real reason had been the change he'd experienced over the past *month*.

With Lily.

For Lily.

Because although she'd thought she wasn't good

enough for him, *he* was the one who had needed to work to be good enough for *her*.

His actions two days ago had shown him he still wasn't good enough for her.

Now, he didn't know why sticking to his plan had been so important to him. Of *course* he still wanted the opportunity to make up for his mistakes. Rugby—the Shadows—had been there for him when he hadn't had anything, and he would do all he could to show his gratitude for that. But since the night they'd spent at the beach restaurant he'd been resisting his feelings for Lily.

He hadn't been acknowledging it, but he'd changed—and that was because of his feelings for her. Feelings he now knew had grown with every moment he'd spent enjoying her company and her uncertain feistiness.

Her point of view had always given him something to think about. And he had genuinely enjoyed seeing how her mind, eager and quick to learn, grasped the aspects of business that he'd taught her.

He'd never been interested in relationships. When he'd discovered rugby—when he'd discovered he was *good* at it—it had become all he'd been able to think about. It had been easier to focus his attention on work than on relationships. Than on love.

Part of him realised now that it was because of the fear witnessing his parents' relationship had instilled in him. And maybe that was why he'd clung to his plan instead of opening up to Lily. It had *still* been easier to focus on work, on things that didn't force him out of his comfort zone.

But Lily had forced herself out of *her* comfort zone to take part in his plan. She'd put herself in the public eye despite her insecurities for *him*. Before she'd really known him. Just because it had been important to *him*.

And he didn't even have the courage to admit that he loved her.

He didn't deny it any more. He was in love with Lily. It still terrified him, but the past two days had shown him something even more terrifying—a life without her.

The fear of that thought had been eclipsed by excitement now. By hope.

She'd always seen a side of him that no one else had bothered to see. He'd known that the moment she'd said those things about him on the talk show. And he knew that was something special. He'd fought for years for the world to see something *she* had seen within twenty-four hours.

Lily had told him she knew how hard he fought for the things he wanted.

It was time he showed her that he wanted *her*.

CHAPTER TWENTY

LILY FLUCTUATED BETWEEN the devastation that had her spending hours in bed and a busyness that had resulted in a spotless house and a fridge filled with food she knew she would have to share with Caitlyn and her parents—as soon as she'd built up the courage to see any of them and explain what had happened with Jacques.

She hadn't heard from him since that night on the beach, but whenever the phone rang her heart jumped with the hope. And then she would see that it wasn't his name or number—like now, when her display showed Caitlyn's name—and she would sink back into the devastation.

'Hello?'

'Wow, you sound terrible.'

'Thanks, Cait.'

'Not in the best of moods, are you?'

Caitlyn's cheery voice grated on her, and Lily clenched her jaw.

'Aren't you supposed to be engaged or something?'

The annoyance turned into devastation once more.

'Yes,' she hiccupped.

'I know it wasn't real, but I saw a clip of it on television again this morning—it's been on about every hour since it happened—and it looked really sweet. Not as sweet as *my* proposal, of course, but then, mine was real—'

'It *was* really sweet,' Lily interrupted, not in the mood for her friend's energy. 'Listen, Caitlyn, I'm not feeling—'

'Actually, Lil, I'm calling for a reason.' There was a pause. 'I'm worried about Nathan. He hasn't been... Well, he hasn't been himself for the past few days. And I know it has something to do with him wanting to smooth things over between his father and Jacques.'

'Yeah, their dad was at Jacques's charity event.'

Caitlyn sighed. 'I know. He wouldn't tell me anything about it.'

'Probably because it didn't go well.'

'I thought so. I heard Jacques was staying at his beach flat so I came by, hoping we could talk, but he isn't here. Could you...? Could you please come by and open up for me? I don't want to wait outside his flat and risk the chance of being branded as "the other woman" if a photographer sees me.'

'You don't know when he'll be back?' Her heart thumped at the prospect of running into him.

'No...please, Lil.' Caitlyn's voice had gone hoarse. 'I'm really worried about Nathan.'

Lily's resistance melted. She couldn't leave her friend in the lurch. 'I'm on my way.'

She clicked off the phone and dragged herself to the bathroom. She showered, shoved her hair into a bun on the top of her head, and stared at her clothing options.

She was engaged, after all. She couldn't look the way she felt. The thought had her selecting a pretty white and pink floral dress and adding a pair of pink button-shaped earrings.

Twenty minutes later she was walking towards Caitlyn at Jacques's flat.

'You're a life-saver,' Caitlyn said as soon as she saw Lily.

'Sure,' Lily answered, and handed her friend the key. 'You can let yourself out.'

'I won't need the key. Jacques can let me out.' Caitlyn frowned. 'Besides, don't *you* need it?'

'I…'

She'd wanted to give Caitlyn the key and escape as soon as she could, but she couldn't answer Caitlyn's question without telling her the truth. She didn't quite have the energy for that.

'Yeah, of course. I'll just let you in, then.'

She took the key back and pushed open the door.

And froze when she saw Jacques.

His gorgeous face was set in a serious expression, his muscular body clothed in fitted black pants and a light blue shirt. He held a gift-wrapped box in his hands, and she idly wondered if it was for her.

And then she began to put the pieces together. Caitlyn's cheerful tone at the beginning of their telephone conversation, the fact that she didn't look nearly as upset as she'd sounded earlier.

'You missed your calling,' she told her friend.

'I'm sorry, Lil.' Caitlyn had the grace to look chagrined. 'It was a favour. For family.'

With one last apologetic look she left. Leaving Lily alone with Jacques.

She closed the door behind her, not wanting anyone to witness whatever was going to happen between them.

'Thank you for staying.'

'Did I have a choice?'

'I… I didn't know if you would have come if I'd asked.'

'I don't know if I would have either.'

Everything inside her was coiled and twisted. She didn't know what to do to make it go away.

'I was hoping we could talk,' he said, and took a step closer.

'About what?' Then she realised what the day was. 'You made your bid today.'

When he nodded, she set her handbag on the couch.

'How did it go? Or are they still making their decision?'

'I got it.'

'Congratulations.'

'Thank you,' he answered, but something in his tone sounded off. 'I really mean that. None of this would have been possible without you.'

'Then why don't you sound happy? It's everything you've ever wanted, isn't it?'

'I thought so. Until I got it and it didn't make me feel the way I thought it would.'

'I don't understand.'

He set the gift down on the coffee table and took another step towards her. She took a step back, unsure whether she would be able to handle it if he came any closer.

His eyes dimmed at her movement, and he shoved his hands into his pockets.

'When you got your shop...did it make all the trouble you'd gone through worth it?'

'You already know the answer to that.'

'Humour me.'

She took a deep breath. 'It felt like it was worth it at first. When I signed the lease on the property...when I decorated it. It was mine. But then... But then reality set in, and I couldn't escape what I'd done to get it.'

'And then it didn't seem worth it any more?'

'For a while. But since I met you things have been

going better. I've told myself I'll pay back the money, and that's made it a little easier to live with myself.'

'When did you make that decision?'

'Two nights ago.'

His eyes searched her face, as though he was looking for something there, and she shifted her weight. Tucked a curl behind her ear.

'Do things…not seem worth it any more to you?' she asked.

He smiled, but she could see the touch of sadness behind his eyes.

'Not so much, no.'

'Why not?'

'Because I sacrificed something much more important to get it.'

Though her heart-rate spiked, she asked, 'What?'

He didn't answer her for a moment, and Lily thought she'd been foolish to ask.

'I told you…you distracted me from my plan. And I meant it. I'd spent years fixated on making a name for myself other than the bad one the world had given me.' He paused. 'When I heard the club was going to be sold I was sure that it would be my chance.'

'I know all of this.'

'Yeah, you do. But you don't know that the reason I was successful in the end was *you*. Not because you helped my reputation—I think we could have chosen anyone else for that and my reputation would have improved.'

This time she didn't move back when he took a step forward.

'I succeeded because *you*, Lily Newman, showed me how to be someone I've been trying to be for years in one month.'

Speechless, she watched as he walked back to the table and picked up the box. She took it from him wordlessly.

'What...?' She cleared her throat when she heard the hoarseness of her voice. 'What is it?'

'Open it. Please.'

It was a plea, and though there was a part of her that was still in shock she was helpless to resist it. She tore the paper open with shaking hands, opened the box and felt the pieces of her heart that were already broken turn into a million more.

He'd given her a beautiful picture frame—wooden and hand-made. She recognised Caitlyn's artistry in it, and knew her friend had created it with Lily in mind. But it wasn't the frame that had Lily choked up. It was the picture it held.

It was a photograph of the exact moment she'd told herself to focus on for the past two days. The moment she recalled when she wanted to think of something happy. When she was brave enough to face what she had lost.

It was a picture taken at the charity event, of when Jacques had proposed to her. He was on his knee, looking up at her with an emotion on his face that was similar to the one it held now. She traced his face, and then looked at her own. Looked at the light, at the hope that shone in her eyes. She saw her eyes focused only on him, though there were so many people looking at her.

When a sob threatened, she put the lid back on the box. 'Why would you give me this?' she rasped, shaken.

'I told you that night that I wished you could see yourself the way I saw you. This picture *shows* you how I see you.'

'I don't know what you want me to see, Jacques,' she said desperately. 'I can't tell what that look on your face is.'

He lifted her chin, forcing her to look at him.

'It's love, Lily. I love you.'
And he kissed her.

He'd thought saying the words would be hard. But once he'd seen her they had come effortlessly. He'd kissed her because he'd been able to tell she didn't believe him. And he'd thought maybe if he could show her...

The moment his lips touched hers there was no more thinking. No more rationalising. He should have known that by now, and yet he was constantly surprised by the way her kiss could consume him.

By the way her *taste* could consume him.

After days of uncertainty—of wondering if he'd ever be consumed by that taste again—he felt more urgency, more greed than he would have liked. For a moment he considered allowing it. He considered letting passion dictate the kiss. But he wanted to show her more than passion. He wanted to show her that there was more than the attraction he'd claimed had always been between them.

She already knew about that. What she *didn't* know about was his love for her. What she didn't know was the intimacy he craved to have with her.

Slowly he deepened the kiss, and with each movement he showed her. With each stroke of his tongue, with each caress of his hands, he opened his heart to her. He showed her that he was hers, and only hers.

And for the first time he discovered that love was more potent than any attraction.

'Stop!' she said breathlessly as she pushed him away.

Somehow they'd ended up against the wall, and when he moved back he wished *he'd* had it behind him to steady him. 'What's wrong?'

'What's *wrong*?' she repeated. 'Jacques, you've had my best friend trick me into coming here. You tell me you got your club, but that it hasn't made you happy. And then you give me this gift, tell me you love me, and kiss me until I don't know who I am...'

Her chest heaved, but he couldn't tell if it was from their kiss or her words.

'You've got what you wanted and it hasn't made you feel the way you wanted it to. So...so maybe you're just moving on to the next thing. What happens if this—if I—don't make you happy? Do you just move on again? Because that...well, it won't work for me.'

'We weren't even a real couple and you made me happier than I've ever been, Lily.' He took her hands in his. 'I know you're worried that this is a rash decision for me, but it isn't. I haven't been able to stop thinking about you.'

He could see that he wasn't convincing her, and panic gripped his heart. But he took a deep breath and reminded himself that he always did whatever it took to get what he wanted. That meant that he needed to fight for Lily.

And *that* meant laying it all on the line.

'I resisted it from the moment we had dinner on that beach and I saw the person you really were. I resisted it through every dinner after that, through every event when I saw you fight against your insecurities. When I saw you overcome them.'

He took a deep breath.

'I fought it because I'd seen what a terrible relationship looked like. I was terrified that I would be like my father—that whatever relationship I was in would turn out to be like my parents. So I stayed away from them.'

'And had multiple partners instead?'

He winced. 'Yeah.'

'So what changed?'

He could tell he had her attention now, and the panic began to subside. 'I met you.'

'As simple as that?'

'As *complicated* as that. I've told you that you changed me, Lily. I mean it. Fear kept me from telling you this before, but I love you.'

Her eyes shone with tears, and her voice was hoarse when she asked, 'And this is not because you're looking for the high you hoped to get when you heard you'd got the club? I'm sorry it didn't feel the way you wanted it to, but…but that can't be the reason you've realised you love me.'

'Not that alone, no,' he agreed. 'I realised I loved you when you called me out on the beach.'

'You love me,' she repeated.

'I do.'

Her eyes began to shine with that hope he'd seen when he'd proposed to her. So he took the box from her hand, opened it again, and handed the frame to her.

'What do you see in that picture?'

'You're proposing.'

'What do you see on my face?'

Tears gleamed in her eyes when she looked at him. 'Is it…is it love?'

He set a hand under her chin, brought her head up to look at him. 'Tell me what you see on my face now, Lily.'

'You mean it?' A tear ran down her cheek. 'Don't do this if you don't mean it.'

'I *do* mean it,' he said quietly, and lowered his hands to her arms. 'Do you want to know what *I* see in that picture, Lil?' He didn't wait for an answer. 'I see a beautiful, kind, caring woman. One who sacrificed her own insecurities to help someone get what they thought they needed.'

He pulled her closer to him.

'I see a woman who has fought to overcome all the things life has thrown at her. Who has used her failures, her mistakes, as lessons. Who showed *me* how to do that too.'

His arms went around her waist, and he closed the distance between them until she was gently pressed to his body.

'I don't want to make *this* mistake, though, Lily. Because I don't know how I'd come back from it. I don't know how I could learn from it when it would be the worst mistake of my life.'

'I didn't know how I could learn from it either,' she whispered. 'I told myself that I could use it as a lesson to be better in the future, but I didn't know how.'

'So we won't make this mistake?'

'No, we won't.'

She looked at him with those beautiful eyes, more piercing now after her tears.

'I love you, Jacques.'

He rested his forehead on hers. 'I've never heard anything that's made me happier in my life.' He took another moment to appreciate it, and then he said, 'I could never imagine being married to someone after seeing what my parents went through. But that's because I'd never loved anyone. And then I met you—I fell in love with you—and I imagined it all so easily. In fact I can't *stop* thinking about it.'

He held his breath, hoping she understood what he'd meant.

'Me either.'

It wasn't the answer he'd hoped for, but the words sounded like trumpets in his ears.

He had a chance.

'I think about a future with you,' she said. 'I look at this gorgeous ring—even though it's pretend—and it undoes every resolution of mine to move on. It undoes every thought of mine that I *can* move on.'

She paused.

'I always thought I didn't deserve the good things in life. And I'd accepted it.'

'You didn't accept what I offered the other night.'

She smiled. 'That was *your* fault. You showed me that settling for anything less than what I wanted wasn't right. Every time I thought something demeaning about myself I heard your voice telling me to snap out of it. Or reminding me of all the things I've achieved. I wouldn't have been able to survive with just a part of you, Jacques. I wanted *all* of you.'

Her eyes flashed with uncertainty, and then the look was replaced with boldness.

'And I think maybe I *deserve* all of you.'

'You do, my love,' he said in relief. 'I'm the one who doesn't deserve *you*.'

'No, Jacques. We're stronger than that now. Together we're stronger. And we deserve each other.'

'Say it again, Lily. Tell me you love me again.'

'I love you.'

She'd barely said the words before his lips were on hers again. This time there were no reservations. This time there was passion. There was greed. There was urgency. But there was also love and intimacy. He gave just as much as he took, his passion fuelled by their acknowledged feelings. By their love.

And then he pulled back.

'I love you too.'

With those words all the turmoil inside her was calmed. All the insecurities faded. And she believed that she deserved this happiness. She deserved this happiness with the man she loved.

'You're a pretty lucky man, Mr Brookes,' she said, looking at the picture again. Now looking at it didn't hurt. 'Some people would say you have it all.'

'Those people would be right,' he replied, grinning. He pulled her in for a hug, his head resting on hers. 'Though you have to admit *you're* pretty lucky too.'

Her cheek rested on his chest, the picture still in her right hand, and she smiled. 'Oh, I know I am. Haven't you read the papers? *I'm* the one who tamed Bad-Boy Brookes.'

He chuckled. 'Yeah, you did. And I'm looking forward to a lifetime of it.'

Her heart sped up and she pulled back, setting the picture on the table.

'Do you mean…?'

'You can't possibly be surprised.' He smiled. 'How do you like that ring?'

'I'm pretty in love with it.' Her heart bursting, she asked one more time. 'Do you *really* mean it?'

'With all my heart, Lily. I can go down on one knee again if it would convince you?'

Lily looked at the picture again, saw the expression on his face. The real one since the emotion she hadn't been able to identify before now had a name. And then she looked at her own face again, and her eyes filled with tears.

'It was real, wasn't it?' she whispered.

'It was, but I'd like to ask you again anyway.'

She smiled when he went down on one knee, this time holding her hand with the diamond ring on it instead of inside its box.

'I love you, Lily. You will *always* be my real redemption. Will you marry me?'

'I can't imagine wanting anything else more.'

He grabbed her, twirled her around. And when they kissed Lily knew that the only thing that would define them in future would be their love for one another.

* * * * *

If you loved this story, check out
A MARRIAGE WORTH SAVING by Therese Beharrie.
Available now!

If you're looking forward to indulging in
another proposal of convenience story,
featuring an enigmatic sheikh, then you'll love
SARAH AND THE SECRET SHEIKH
by Michelle Douglas.

MILLS & BOON®
Hardback – August 2017

ROMANCE

An Heir Made in the Marriage Bed	Anne Mather
The Prince's Stolen Virgin	Maisey Yates
Protecting His Defiant Innocent	Michelle Smart
Pregnant at Acosta's Demand	Maya Blake
The Secret He Must Claim	Chantelle Shaw
Carrying the Spaniard's Child	Jennie Lucas
A Ring for the Greek's Baby	Melanie Milburne
Bought for the Billionaire's Revenge	Clare Connelly
The Runaway Bride and the Billionaire	Kate Hardy
The Boss's Fake Fiancée	Susan Meier
The Millionaire's Redemption	Therese Beharrie
Captivated by the Enigmatic Tycoon	Bella Bucannon
Tempted by the Bridesmaid	Annie O'Neil
Claiming His Pregnant Princess	Annie O'Neil
A Miracle for the Baby Doctor	Meredith Webber
Stolen Kisses with Her Boss	Susan Carlisle
Encounter with a Commanding Officer	Charlotte Hawkes
Rebel Doc on Her Doorstep	Lucy Ryder
The CEO's Nanny Affair	Joss Wood
Tempted by the Wrong Twin	Rachel Bailey

MILLS & BOON®
Large Print – August 2017

ROMANCE

The Italian's One-Night Baby	Lynne Graham
The Desert King's Captive Bride	Annie West
Once a Moretti Wife	Michelle Smart
The Boss's Nine-Month Negotiation	Maya Blake
The Secret Heir of Alazar	Kate Hewitt
Crowned for the Drakon Legacy	Tara Pammi
His Mistress with Two Secrets	Dani Collins
Stranded with the Secret Billionaire	Marion Lennox
Reunited by a Baby Bombshell	Barbara Hannay
The Spanish Tycoon's Takeover	Michelle Douglas
Miss Prim and the Maverick Millionaire	Nina Singh

HISTORICAL

Claiming His Desert Princess	Marguerite Kaye
Bound by Their Secret Passion	Diane Gaston
The Wallflower Duchess	Liz Tyner
Captive of the Viking	Juliet Landon
The Spaniard's Innocent Maiden	Greta Gilbert

MEDICAL

Their Meant-to-Be Baby	Caroline Anderson
A Mummy for His Baby	Molly Evans
Rafael's One Night Bombshell	Tina Beckett
Dante's Shock Proposal	Amalie Berlin
A Forever Family for the Army Doc	Meredith Webber
The Nurse and the Single Dad	Dianne Drake

MILLS & BOON®
Hardback – September 2017

ROMANCE

The Tycoon's Outrageous Proposal	Miranda Lee
Cipriani's Innocent Captive	Cathy Williams
Claiming His One-Night Baby	Michelle Smart
At the Ruthless Billionaire's Command	Carole Mortimer
Engaged for Her Enemy's Heir	Kate Hewitt
His Drakon Runaway Bride	Tara Pammi
The Throne He Must Take	Chantelle Shaw
The Italian's Virgin Acquisition	Michelle Conder
A Proposal from the Crown Prince	Jessica Gilmore
Sarah and the Secret Sheikh	Michelle Douglas
Conveniently Engaged to the Boss	Ellie Darkins
Her New York Billionaire	Andrea Bolter
The Doctor's Forbidden Temptation	Tina Beckett
From Passion to Pregnancy	Tina Beckett
The Midwife's Longed-For Baby	Caroline Anderson
One Night That Changed Her Life	Emily Forbes
The Prince's Cinderella Bride	Amalie Berlin
Bride for the Single Dad	Jennifer Taylor
A Family for the Billionaire	Dani Wade
Taking Home the Tycoon	Catherine Mann

0817 GEN STD HB

MILLS & BOON®
Large Print – September 2017

ROMANCE

The Sheikh's Bought Wife	Sharon Kendrick
The Innocent's Shameful Secret	Sara Craven
The Magnate's Tempestuous Marriage	Miranda Lee
The Forced Bride of Alazar	Kate Hewitt
Bound by the Sultan's Baby	Carol Marinelli
Blackmailed Down the Aisle	Louise Fuller
Di Marcello's Secret Son	Rachael Thomas
Conveniently Wed to the Greek	Kandy Shepherd
His Shy Cinderella	Kate Hardy
Falling for the Rebel Princess	Ellie Darkins
Claimed by the Wealthy Magnate	Nina Milne

HISTORICAL

The Secret Marriage Pact	Georgie Lee
A Warriner to Protect Her	Virginia Heath
Claiming His Defiant Miss	Bronwyn Scott
Rumours at Court (Rumors at Court)	Blythe Gifford
The Duke's Unexpected Bride	Lara Temple

MEDICAL

Their Secret Royal Baby	Carol Marinelli
Her Hot Highland Doc	Annie O'Neil
His Pregnant Royal Bride	Amy Ruttan
Baby Surprise for the Doctor Prince	Robin Gianna
Resisting Her Army Doc Rival	Sue MacKay
A Month to Marry the Midwife	Fiona McArthur

MILLS & BOON®

Why shop at millsandboon.co.uk?

Each year, thousands of romance readers find their perfect read at millsandboon.co.uk. That's because we're passionate about bringing you the very best romantic fiction. Here are some of the advantages of shopping at www.millsandboon.co.uk:

* **Get new books first**—you'll be able to buy your favourite books one month before they hit the shops

* **Get exclusive discounts**—you'll also be able to buy our specially created monthly collections, with up to 50% off the RRP

* **Find your favourite authors**—latest news, interviews and new releases for all your favourite authors and series on our website, plus ideas for what to try next

* **Join in**—once you've bought your favourite books, don't forget to register with us to rate, review and join in the discussions

Visit **www.millsandboon.co.uk**
for all this and more today!